Abilene

a novel by

Dare DeLano

MINT HILL BOOKS
MAIN STREET RAG PUBLISHING COMPANY
CHARLOTTE, NORTH CAROLINA

Library of Congress Control Number: 2023940738

ISBN: 978-1-59948-966-7

Produced in the United States of America

Mint Hill Books
Main Street Rag Publishing Company
PO Box 690100
Charlotte, NC 28227
www.MainStreetRag.com

For my father
who has always been there for me

PROLOGUE
Lenora (Len)

Moonchild, Granny called me. For I was born when the moon was full, in a flat ranch house in Abilene, Texas. Granny always said that on account of that moon, I would move with the rhythm of nature—that my intuition was strong and that I would know about the insides of people—see things in my head before others watched them happen in the world. She stroked my hair and taught me songs with no words.

We'd sit out on the screen porch before supper, shucking corn and shelling butter beans, the wind wrapped around us like a blanket. She'd tell me stories about her cousin Dweasel who could speak in tongues and heal people just by touching 'em. Granny'd stare right at me, squint her eyes and say, "You got it too, honey, I can tell." And as I looked at her strong, wrinkled face and watched her strip an ear of corn clean in three sharp tugs, I believed her with my whole heart.

And I knew in my bones she was right. For often, with the first winds of morning, I could feel how the day was gonna go. I could feel the long, strange cry of a wolf, or the glorious scream of the eagle, circling. At the beach I could hear the sailors' words as they were carried along in cries of the seagulls.

I knew someday that wind would bring me news of my daddy. For although I'd never seen him, I knew his face like it was a part of me, memorized from the only picture I had of him. Not a nice, framed picture on the mantle like at some people's houses—I had a dog-eared piece of a polaroid, almost thirteen years old, that I kept in my underwear drawer.

For as long as I could remember I'd been waiting for that day, waiting for word of my daddy to come to me, so that big empty space inside of me would be filled. And I kept waiting.

By the time I turned twelve years old, I was mighty impatient.

CHAPTER 1

Len (2001)

The sun is just beginning to peek over the horizon, and the morning is cool and dry. As I open screen the door and breathe in the air, I know there is something on the horizon, something coming my way.

I slip on my muck boots and head out to the barn. I don't ride the perimeter every morning—only when I feel the darkness creeping in. No one else seems to notice—the dark clouds that press in from outside the ranch. But there is a song that sits inside of me, deep and waiting. And when I ride the perimeter it flows, wordless like waves out into the world, and those dark clouds just roll on along and leave us all alone.

I creak open the barn door and step inside. The horses are softly munching their hay, and the air smells of sweet feed and dust.

"Mornin' Pea," Walter says, handing me a soft sticky bun with powdered sugar on it.

"Thanks." I take a bite, the sugar puffing in a small cloud as I breathe on it. Most mornings Walter has something for me—a thick slice of warm cornbread, a peach so ripe it drools down my chin when I bite into it. We don't talk this early in the morning, we just munch right along with the horses.

Walter turns back to mucking stalls, whistling soft and low. He wears his big work overalls, a handkerchief shoved into his side pocket. There's already one big smudge mark across his forehead from where he's wiped the sweat away, his skin like a board just after you put shellac over it and it's not yet dry.

He moves slower lately, sits in the shade earlier in the day for his break, and I try not to think about that. I finish my sticky bun, lick my fingers, and start to tack up Cyclops. I can ride the other horses when someone's with me, but if I'm going out on the trail by myself, I have to take Cyclops. I don't think he has ever moved at any pace faster than a slow trot in his whole life, but I don't care. He never spooks, no matter what.

I saddle the horse quickly, for I can feel an extra tension in the air, pressing in around me. Cyclops watches me with his good eye as I put away the brushes and tighten his girth.

We set out towards the northwest corner, crickets chirping and the smell of sage all around us. I ride the dirt trail the ranch hands use—it runs out to the northwest corner and hugs the fence line. Our ranch is a hundred and forty acres of flat brown land. A few cactus plants grow up out of the cracked earth, their bulbous leaves sucking up all the moisture for miles around. Here and there are a few rambling bushes, some tumbleweed, and tufts of crabgrass wherever it will grow. Cattle graze year round, although sometimes in the summer it gets so brown we have to feed them hay and oats until we get some rain.

Our house is an oasis in the middle of all that brown. Most folks have the Texas shade trees around their homes—Texas Lilacs and Chinkapin Oaks. That and a little green grass surrounding the house, and maybe some flowers for color. But our house is different. We've had folks from the Taylor County Horticultural Society spend afternoons examining the plants, making notes about what's growing where, and even taking little samples of dirt away to run tests on it. 'Cause around our house the landscape is green and lush, with Japanese primroses, Louisiana irises, ostrich fern feathers, and the whole of the side yard covered with creeping jenny. And in the middle of it all, rising impossible and lovely against the Texas sky, is the banana tree Ma found one morning years ago, left on the doorstep like an abandoned baby, small and thin and in a pot. They've never found any explanation, those horticulturalists. It just seems that no matter what Ma decides to plant, it will grow as if we are in the middle of a rainforest. But not along the perimeter. Where I ride, it is brown and dry and barren.

Once I get to the far end of the ranch, I turn and ride along the fence line. As usual, I can see the darks clouds on the horizon, rolling toward me. I close my eyes and look deep inside. I feel a shimmer, and when I send that shimmer out into the world, it is a song no one else can hear. When I let it out, the clouds recede, and I know we are safe another day. I don't actually know what would happen if the clouds crept all the way in, but I have my theories. Because the closer they get, the less Ma laughs and darker her day. Sadness is coming for Ma, and I'm just doing my part to keep it at bay.

Cyclops and I are slow and steady. The north fence is mended, the milking shed is bustling with activity. Nothing is out of sorts. Until I turn for home. That is when I see clouds I've never seen before—right over the house.

I saw a cyclone once. It raced along the open fields and Ma and I ran for cover to watch it pass even though it was miles away. But these clouds are different, they are willowy, and they disappear almost entirely when I look directly at them. There's a deep humming sound that I can feel through my whole body. Suddenly everything feels a little unbalanced, like the whole world is leaning slightly. And I know that I need to get home.

I quicken my pace, pushing Cyclops to his limit, which is maddeningly slow. I can see Aunt Cisley's car in the driveway, and I don't even brush Cyclops before I put him back in his stall. I have never known Cisley to be up this early in the morning.

The air around the front door is so thick it stops me before I put my hand on the doorknob. It is dense and hot, and there is a pulsing noise that fills my ears, so I know there is something going on they don't want me to hear. Instead, I head to my place under the house. I crawl into the dark space, smelling the rawness of the wood where it meets the earth. The forgotten space.

A spider crawls across the board beside me, within inches of my forearm, making the hair on my arm stand up.

"Go away," I whisper. He twitches his brown spindly legs and moves on.

I hear only murmurs, not words, so I keep crawling right up underneath the porch swing and settle myself in.

"I don't see anything crazy about it," Aunt Cisley is saying. "She just walked into her house and found them in the middle of it. They weren't even in the bedroom—they were in her living room. Broad daylight and they're doin' it right on the new couch she just had delivered last week." Her voice is shrill. "If I walked home to that sight, and I had a gun in my purse, I can't say I wouldn't have done the same thing."

Her bracelets tinkle, and I picture Cisley stirring more sugar into her tea. "Sorry Cora, I didn't mean it like that," she says softly. I figure Ma must have given her some kind of look on account of Aunt Cisley is married to Ma's brother, my Uncle Bo.

"Shit," Ma says. "Who would have thought she had it in her?"

"I always said there was something about that Roger I didn't trust. I always said steer clear of him." I can tell by the rhythm in Granny's voice she is in her rocking chair.

They are silent for a while—there is just the soft squeak of the rocking chair and the sound of ice cubes against a spoon.

The phone rings, sharp and insistent, and footsteps head into the foyer. Ma calls Cisley to the phone. I strain to hear her over the pounding in my ears. Ma says, low as if she is talking to me, "Roger's still unconscious. They're not sure if he's going to make it." It is the worry in Ma's voice that brings a hot flush to my face. The news that my uncle might die does not touch me so deep—he isn't truly an uncle, he's my Uncle Bo's brother-in-law, and I've never liked him much anyway.

Cisley returns to the porch. "Mama wants me to come with her to the jailhouse. I don't know what help she thinks I'm gonna be." She lets out a sharp little laugh, almost a bark. "Jean's the smart one, not me. Unless she needs a new hairdo to go with her prison jumpsuit, I can't see what good it's gonna do for me to be there."

"Your mother doesn't need you to be smart right now," Granny says. "She just needs you to be there."

When I hear car keys jangling, I crawl back out from the porch and dust myself off. Ma is already on the front stoop with Cisley, and she narrows her eyes at me, suspicious.

"Len, can you go on out to the barn and make sure the mares have water?"

"Walter already watered the horses, it's past seven." I stare hard at her. She knows I am asking what happened.

Ma raises her eyebrows at me.

Cisley shrugs and pulls open the door to her car. She squints, holding up a hand with long pink fingernails to shield her eyes as she looks toward the house. She tosses her head and her blond curls bounce. "She's gonna hear about it sooner or later, you might as well get it over with."

Ma sighs. "It's Jean," she says, her voice sounding tired. "I don't know how else to say this, but apparently last night she shot your Uncle Roger. He's in the hospital, and we just don't know yet how bad his injuries are."

The morning sun is just beginning to send its heat out over us, and I listen to the calls of the sparrows and killdeers coming from the dense leaves of the river birch tree overhead. I picture Aunt Jean, thin and plain but with a fire inside of her that I can always see so clearly no matter how quiet she is. But when I try to picture Uncle Roger, things start to go blurry. Ma is at the edge of the porch saying something to Cisley, and suddenly the edges of everything merge together—I don't see separate shapes anymore, it has all become one. The song rises inside me until I can no longer keep it in. I am not sending it out on purpose like I do when I ride the perimeter—it is rising and singing all by itself. I can feel it, the way you can feel a drumbeat if it's loud enough, and the world starts to swirl around me. Instead of the ranch, I see Uncle Roger in front of me. He is lying in a hospital bed, and I know somehow that I have to visit him there. Then it is gone suddenly, and the world goes black. My limbs feel limp and my head spins, and somewhere, down a long tunnel I heard Granny calling, "Cora, get an icepack, quick!"

CHAPTER 2

Jean (2001)

The pastor looks like he could still be in high school. He has pimply skin and I bet he's never shaved a day in his life. He sits across from me in my cell, his eyes filled with pity. He talks about the Lord, and how he can forgive all, and when he uses the word 'repent,' it is about all I can do to keep from rolling my eyes.

I take the bible he gives me and I put it on my cot. But I don't bow my head with him when he starts to pray. And I don't make the sign of the cross even though my hand itches to do it. And when the guards come to get me, I stand up and walk out of my cell without saying goodbye. When I was a girl, I used to go to church every Sunday, no matter what. But I reckon by now, I am pretty far past saving.

I walk, right in step with the guards. It's damp and cold, and our footsteps echo for what seems like forever. On my left is little Bobby Shuster, all grown up. He used to mow our lawn sometimes in the summer when Roger was feeling generous and lazy. On the other side is Polly McKenzy's son, Nate. We walk into a large room, empty except for two small card tables and some folding chairs. The clank of the door as it closes is so loud I nearly jump out of my skin. Bobby puts his hand on my shoulder—gentle-like, as if he is afraid I will break.

"Just wait here one minute Mrs. Goodson. Your lawyer's on his way."

I nod and stand right where I am, but he pulls out one of the folding chairs in front of the table and motions me toward it. I sit. My hands are in my lap, folded, so that the handcuffs dig into my skin just a little where my wrists rest on my thighs. My orange jumpsuit surprises me. I don't remember changing into it.

"Has it just been one night?" I ask Nate softly.

He looks at me, not understanding.

"Have I been here in jail only one night?" I ask again.

His whole face softens and I think I see a little worry there. "Yes Ma'am." He answers, nodding gently. "They brought you in yesterday, right after..."

I nod. That's what I thought.

The public defender, Jonny Barkly, enters and sets his worn briefcase on the table. I remember him from when I lived with my folks still and went to the church on High Street. He was always kind. His eyes are still kind. But he is puffing as though he's just walked up three flights of stairs. His gray suit bulges around his middle. It matches the hair around his temples. He pulls out the chair across from me, sits down, and leans forward, arms on the table. Suddenly, I remember this same scene—Jonny sitting across a table just like this and talking to me, serious. Was it yesterday?

"The Judge granted you bail, Jean," he says, his breath becoming steady again. "But he set it a little higher than I wanted." He pauses. "Three hundred thousand. They'll let you call your ma. Have her get in touch with the bondsman. See what they can do. It might be they could post that bond with only five or ten thousand down."

I try to smile. Ain't no way me or my ma has that kind of money sitting around.

"I know I explained how it all works. But I want to make sure you understand."

"I understand it Jonny." I look him in the eye this time. "I seen my mama in shock once after she wrecked her car. I expect that's all it is with me right now. I ain't off my rocker like ya'll think. I reckon I'm just in shock is all."

Jonny nods. "I think that is exactly what it is Jean." His face relaxes a little.

"Well, from here we just need to wait a bit, see what happens," he says. "Right now, like I said, they charged you with second degree assault and attempted murder. But once they know whether Roger has…" his voice trails off. He tries again, "Once they're sure Roger's going to be OK, they'll drop the attempted murder charge. I'm sure of it."

"I understand Jonny," I say again. But I don't, not really.

"The preliminary hearing is set for three weeks from now. You're lucky—that's real quick. I worked it out for you to stay here in town until then, instead of going up to County."

I shrug. I don't expect it makes much difference to me which place they send me.

"At County you can only have visitors once a week—on Saturdays. Here, it is a little more flexible." He exchanges looks with Bobby and Nate.

"I don't want anybody to see me in here," I say quickly. "I don't want Lucas to see me in here."

"Now Jean." He sounds like he's talking to a child. "You might not like the idea of your family seeing you like this, but they're your family, and they'll want to come. They know you're here. You can't hide it by not seeing them."

I let out a long breath and ask, "When would they come?"

"Day after tomorrow."

I don't speak for a long while. Then slowly I say, "I'll have to check my calendar, but I believe I'm free then."

The men all laugh like I've made a big joke.

"Good," Jonny says, as he stands and reaches down for his briefcase. "Good."

I wonder, as they lead me back to my cell, how long it will take before they know I wasn't being completely honest when I said I wasn't off my rocker.

CHAPTER 3

Jean (2001)

The thing that gets to me most in here is the smell. It creeps in and reaches right inside—like the empty halls at grade school when you have to walk by yourself to class because you were dropped off late. It smells like the trailer in the back of the church where Pastor Thomas lived before they sent him away. Where you would leave the thick warm smell of candles and incense and dark wood and walk in with Father Thomas who would say "can you just help me with my robes a minute," and when you reached to help him he would get all muddled and move around crazy and rubbing on you so you'd back away and run out the door while he grunted.

I reckon it must be the Lysol. Cold concrete and Lysol. It's a lonely smell.

I have been here two days. Forty-eight hours. Two thousand eight hundred and eighty minutes. A helluva lotta seconds.

I pick at the moth-eaten gray blanket that covers the bed. Looks like it's near been pulled apart by folks before me. I am used to being busy. I am used to keeping track of my time, making a list of all the things I have to do so I don't forget. But here, sitting on my tiny cot, there is nothing to do but think. I'd rather I had something to keep my mind from doing too much of that.

There are things I try not to worry about—did I leave dishes in the sink, or a load of laundry in the washer that's going to be all mildew smelly by now? Did someone remember to let the dog out, or has he made a mess all over the living room carpet? And what about the blood? I saw it, red and deep, sinking into the tan carpet by the sofa. I hope Lucas didn't see that. I hope Ma had it covered up good before she brought him back home.

My crazy came in waves—forgetting to pay a bill, getting confused about when I was supposed to pick up Lucas. When it's real bad I can't even remember where the furniture is in our house. I didn't used to be like this. I used to be the smart one, the responsible one who got things done.

I was like that when I first met Roger—I was taking care of things then. Back when I was working at the North Fork Trucking Company. I got that job right out of high school because I was good on the phones, and I could type. If I think about it hard enough, I can still smell the donuts in the break room the day I first met him. I was in early that day. It was quiet—the drivers from the night shift hadn't come in yet, and those on day shift were sittin' in the break room with their coffee.

The boss was in a mood. I walked past his desk quickly so he didn't have time to make some comment about how flat my ass was. I made it to my desk and stashed my purse and the plastic bag with my lunch underneath it. I punched my buttons and talked into my headset all morning, keeping the trucks on target, getting them all where they were supposed to go and making sure they picked up what they were supposed to pick up.

It was just before my lunch break when Roger Goodson came through, dungarees sagging just a little, and winked at me. I turned away as he punched his timecard and told myself not to look up as he stomped his boots back by my desk. But he didn't keep going out the door like usual. He stopped at my desk and waited until I looked up at him.

"You have a nice voice," he said. "Sometimes it can be tough out there all night on the road. It's good to have a nice voice to talk to."

I nodded, feeling the pink come to my cheeks. When the phone rang again, I punched the line and answered it. As I talked on the dispatch line, I refused to look at him, and after a bit he walked away.

For our break that day, Mabel and I took our lunches and sat out on the plastic chairs set out behind the building. "The patio" we called it. With a patch of browned grass, a walnut tree that dropped its leaves and shells all over, and a small table set between plastic chairs. It wasn't grand, but the air was warm and dry, and the sun was muted behind a rare set of clouds.

Mabel took a thermos out of her cooler, and then a large package of tinfoil she unwrapped to reveal fried chicken. Mabel's ma still packed her lunch for her, even putting tinfoil wraps over the ends of the drumsticks so she could eat them without getting her fingers all greasy. Mabel set out her whole lunch and then put a napkin in her lap like she was at a restaurant. The sides of her spilled over the plastic chair so that it looked as if it would barely hold her, but she settled in and daintily picked up the end of a drumstick. I took my sandwich out of my bag and sipped a Mountain Dew from the vending machine.

"I reckon that Roger Goodson fella's a little sweet on you."

"I don't think so, Mabel. I guess it makes sense to come say 'Hi' to somebody in person that you got to talk to when you are out on the road, don't it?"

She shrugged. "Ain't never come by to say 'Hi' to me, and I talk to him on the road too."

I smiled just a little. "He did say I had a nice voice."

"Yeah, but I bet it ain't your voice he was thinking about when he said it." We both laughed, and I allowed myself a moment. A moment of being like the pretty girls in high school.

"Ya think so?"

She nodded, more serious now.

That afternoon I talked to Roger Goodson on the line. He was out on the road to Lubbock and called in.

"Hey there, I'm glad it's you." He said it like we'd known each other forever—like we were old friends.

I kept my phone voice on. "How can I help you?"

He gave a small laugh. "Oh, I'm sure I can think of something."

I didn't say anything to that and he started again. "I think maybe I hear a rattle in the engine."

"Ok," I said. "I can set up a service stop at the next station if you want."

"Maybe," he said. "But now I don't hear it anymore."

I waited.

"Maybe if you just stay on the line a minute it'll come back," he said.

I still didn't say anything.

"Have you ever been to Lubbock?" he asked me.

"No," I replied.

"It sure is pretty out here," he said. "There's this lake I'm gonna pass by in just a few miles. The water is blue and clear, and there's trees you can sit under. Nice place to stop to stretch when you've been at the wheel for six hours."

"Maybe you ought to stop there for a rest—I'll log it in if you want."

"No," he said. "Not today. I want to drop the load and get back tonight."

After a while he asked, "Are you working tonight?"

My stomach did a little flip, and I hid again behind my phone voice. "Not tonight. I came in at four this morning."

"Umm," he said. Then suddenly, "Well, I don't hear that rattle anymore—maybe it was just an old coke bottle in the back."

"OK," I said. "You just call back if you need a service stop after all."

"Yes Ma'am," he said. "Yes I will, Jean." And when he said my name, I felt my heart jump. I told myself it wasn't because of him, but I volunteered for the next shift after mine and ended up staying late after all.

"Are you wearing lipstick?" Mabel asked me when I came back from a restroom break. I smiled and rolled my eyes at her. I was. And I put on the powder pink sweater that Cisley had left behind when she stopped by a few days before. I'd kept it in my desk drawer meaning to bring it to her. Mabel raised her eyebrows. "Hubba Hubba," she said. Then she winked at me, smacked her gum and turned back to her switchboard.

It was well after dark when Roger came into the office. "Sixteen hours," he said to me. "Damn that can make a man ache."

"You should soak your feet in some Epsom Salts," I said. "It should help after a long shift."

"Honey, it ain't rightly my feet that are the achin' part," he said, rubbing his backside just a bit.

His eyes twinkled at me, and I felt somehow that he saw me. Not only that, he made me feel like he liked what he saw.

But now, sitting in this dank cell, I can't know—was my crazy there inside of me, even then? I didn't have any inkling of it yet. Those days seem like a lifetime ago now.

And here is how I know for sure things have gotten as bad as they can get—I have been here two days, in this place built for the worst of society, and in all that time, I ain't even cried. Not once.

CHAPTER 4

Cora (Summer 1988)

T he X was kicking in. Coralee was just beginning to feel the spread of euphoria—that moment where every cell in your body is filled with love and happiness. Her mind was racing so fast there was no way her words could keep pace.

"Tell me more about Nietzsche!" her friend Eric called over the music. But the bass was pulling her—every inch of her skin suddenly wanted to move, not talk.

"Screw you," she laughed. She couldn't stop smiling even if she wanted to. Roger watched, with those hard eyes that made her uncomfortable. She looked away, pretending she didn't notice. She missed the nightlife in Georgetown but she was home for the summer and trying to make the best of it. Roger looked out of place with his Levi's and collared shirt. He'd be right at home at almost any bar in Abilene. But not at the Upstairs Lounge, and certainly not on a Tuesday, when, she had to admit, the crowd was pretty good. Next to him a guy with green spikey hair stood up and danced in place maniacally.

Coralee wanted to finish explaining. She often found herself trying to explain the topic to others—Heidegger's theory of being, or Husserl's embryonic idea of it. Whenever people here in her hometown found out what she studied, she would get the same reaction. *Really?* they would raise their eyebrows in surprise. *Philosophy? At Georgetown?* It was as if she was an alien being, and although she'd lived among them all her life, they had suddenly realized she belonged to an entirely different world. They didn't ask about Heidegger of course, but if pressed to explain what she was studying, that was usually the answer she gave—concrete enough to satisfy most people, but esoteric enough, usually, to discourage further questioning. But for some reason, Eric wanted to know about Nietzsche.

Cora's mind was going a mile a minute, and it was reaching places it couldn't quite go without the drug. She was thinking about experience and existence, about how even science itself could not escape the lens of human experience, how even science could not be approached in a purely objective manner, since it was impossible to come at things from a blank slate— even if we were to have no preconceptions (which, she would often argue to the rationalists, was not actually possible), our perceptions themselves were singular—they may be universal to the human experience, however it was impossible to know whether they were "true" or whether they were merely our perceptions, one perspective in a multidimensional truth.

"It's all about how we think of our lives isn't it? It's the story we tell ourselves at the end of the day that makes us who we are—the story we tell of our lives." She had to yell to be heard over the music. "Isn't that what Shakespeare said anyway— there is no good or bad, but thinking makes it so." She took a sip of her Long Island Iced Tea and used her hands as she talked. "I can tell my story as a victim and elicit sympathy or tell my story as a survivor and draw admiration. Which one do we want? How do we want to be perceived? I am, I suppose, a phenomenologist at heart, even though I proclaim myself to be an existentialist. As always, I come back to Sartre."

Cora knew she was not saying it right, although Eric stared at her, concentrating hard. She could feel the music in her teeth by then. She couldn't talk anymore—she could only smile. She grabbed the green-hair guy by the elbow and pulled him to the dance floor. He was feeling it too—they did not care about each other, did not know each other, but they loved everything together. The orbs and enzymes were aligning so that all of life was good, and Cora was so alive.

She lost track of the minutes, of the hours. She lost track of the number of Long Island Iced Teas her bartender friend slipped her when she made it to the bar. She lost track of the number of Jell-O shots she and her friends threw back while they were on top of the world. But by the time the sun was peeking over the horizon in bloodshot veins, she found herself behind the club puking up a green gelatinous mess. She wiped her mouth with her sleeve and suddenly realized someone was holding her hair back.

She sat back and leaned against the grimy brick of the building. It took a few minutes for his face to come into focus. "Jesus—did I just puke in front of you?"

"Yeah, pretty much."

"Damn it. You're cute too. That's too bad."

"Why is it too bad?"

What is this guy, an idiot or something? she thought. *Too bad brains don't go along with those looks.*

"I'm not an idiot," his voice was a little defensive.

"Shit, did I say that out loud?"

He cocked his head to the side and smiled just a bit.

"Come on," he took Cora's arm, "Let's get you back inside."

"OK." She tried to shift so that her feet were underneath her, but somehow they were not working properly. "That's pretty optimistic of you," she said, sitting back down against the brick.

When he smiled, his whole face lit up.

"Wait—did you just watch me puke?"

He took a deep breath. "Well, this will be quite a story to tell our kids one day, won't it?"

If he would just stay in focus for a little bit it would really help, Cora thought.

"Do I even know you?"

"You just talked to me for like two hours inside. I'm friends with Mike Dobson, I'm crashing on his couch for a few days."

Cora nodded. She knew vaguely who Mike was—a friend of a friend of a friend, but it didn't really seem to matter. The world had stopped spinning, but she didn't quite trust it to stay still while she tried to stand up.

"My name's Edison. It's usually real easy for people to remember."

"I think I probably should just go home," Cora said.

He helped her to a cab. She tried not to notice the feel of his hand on her arm, the electric sensation that she felt long after the cab dropped her off and she stumbled into the old farmhouse, trying not to wake anyone.

CHAPTER 5

Cora (1988)

W hen he walked into the store, Cora hid behind the display. She reminded herself she had no need to be embarrassed—well, ok maybe puking behind the club was a bit much, but it wasn't like she'd slept with him or something. She watched him for a moment, knowing he couldn't see her, as he glanced around the place. His hair was definitely too "Flock of Seagulls" for her. The guys she went for were extremes—shaved heads or mohawks—at the very least dyed or bleached. But when she saw his shoes—Florsheim's, shiny and stitched, worn with black dress slacks despite the heat, something caught in her throat despite her wishes.

She realized she needed to act natural, so she walked behind the counter, not looking his way, as if she didn't see him.

"Hi," he said. His smile was disarming. But he was too much of a pretty-boy for her, she was certain of it.

"Hey," Cora shrugged, as if it were the most normal thing in the world for him to be in the video store.

"What time are you done?" he asked.

She raised her eyebrows. No lead in? No small talk? How was he even so sure she was going to remember who he was?

"Cause, there's this thing," he went on, "this outdoor Cary Grant movie they're showing in Sweetwater, but we'd have to leave in like an hour to make it in time."

"Oh yeah?" she said.

"Yeah."

Looking back later, she could never say why she agreed to go. But she did. On the drive they talked—mostly about bands and clubs in Dallas they'd been to or heard of. She told him how she was going back to her third year at Georgetown after the summer break.

"Yeah, I know," he said. "You told me all about it last night."

"Really? What else did I tell you?"

He got a sneaky smile, raised his eyebrows a little, but said nothing.

She shrugged. "Whatever."

"You told me a lot about all sorts of philosophy," he said grinning.

Cora's roommate at Georgetown, Tessa, was always analyzing her. She told her it was incongruity that Cora relished—wearing her Sisters of Mercy T-shirt and ripped leggings to an Ivy League school—the trappings of blue blood privilege against the rebellion of youth. Tessa liked to point out that it was a tired and overdone rebellion that each new generation believed was its own.

"I just like the music," Cora would always say in her defense. But she knew there was something to what Tessa said. There was a safety in her rebellion. She didn't come from the hallowed halls of an east coast prep school, and she was not a fourth generation Ivy Leaguer, but even Cora saw the irony in her joining the mosh pit and railing against 'the man' when her family owned half the farmland in North Abilene and had for generations. She recognized punk rock was for the street kids in London, but as she insisted to Tessa, she really did like the music. And she loved Cary Grant movies. Had she told him that last night during their epic chat that she didn't remember?

Cora shrugged. "My dad was a philosopher," she said. "Well, it might be that he was really just a hippie, but he sure knew a lot about philosophy."

Edison nodded again. He told her how he just finished his degree in English literature at UT, and how he paid the bills by waiting tables while he wrote plays. He had a killer idea for a screenplay.

"The thing is, I have this agent."

"You have an agent to help you sell your screenplay?"

"No. I have an agent to help me get acting jobs, but he knows all these big-time producers. He says once I get in with them with the acting thing, that's the time to pitch my ideas."

To Cora, the plan sounded overly optimistic, but she just smiled and said, "Cool."

They turned off the freeway onto the narrow road leading to the drive-in. Edison parked the car and popped open the trunk to pull out a blanket and a picnic basket.

"Are you kidding me? You brought an actual picnic basket?"

"Well, yeah, for a picnic."

"OK, if you say so."

There was a large screen set up at one end of the lawn. There was not much of a crowd—some families, some older couples, a few groups of people with lawn chairs and coolers. They walked over to an open area and Cora helped him lay out the blanket. They sat, and as the opening credits started, Edison poured white wine into plastic cups and spread out some cheese and crackers.

"Well, aren't you impressive," Cora said, laughing.

"Thank you, I thought so."

She loved Cary Grant. She loved the era where good was good and idealism prevailed, and her favorite movie of all time was North by Northwest—the tension, the dashed hopes, the intrigue, the heartbreak. It didn't quite fit with her rebel persona, but she didn't care. She was enraptured. By the time the final credits rolled, Cora was leaning back against Edison's legs as he sat with his knees bent.

They packed up the wine bottle and plastic cups, folded up the blanket. As they walked back to the car, he took her hand. She didn't pull it away. And it was like her whole body let out a long slow breath—like she hadn't even known she was waiting for something until that moment.

CHAPTER 6

Len (2001)

W hen I wake, a damp washcloth lies across my forehead.
"It's the moon," Granny says as soon as my eyes open. "You need a sprig of holly under your bed when you sleep." She purses her lips together and runs a weathered hand over my forehead.

"It's not the moon," Ma says. "She's probably just dehydrated again—and she needs to eat something first if she's gonna go riding that early. Here, sit up honey, we made you some tea." She is kneeling beside me, and Granny sits in the armchair next to the coffee table holding a steaming mug.

I push the quilt off my feet and sit up. My vision is clear, but there is still a little hum echoing in my head, making me feel foggy.

"How do you feel, Lady Lazarus?" Ma asks. She takes my hand and squeezes it.

"You know that poem is about suicide, right?"

She blanches. I suspect she hasn't read it since college, but I looked it up last time she called me that.

"Maybe I'm not quoting," she says. Maybe I'm just using the phrase on my own because it fits the context."

Or maybe she just likes to imagine she's still young and wearing black and in college again. I used to think it was normal—I used to figure that everyone's mom went around quoting things like Sylvia Plath or Plato or Shakespeare's sonnets. She doesn't do it to show off. It's more like she is living in a foreign country, and she's just checking to see if anyone else speaks her language.

"Well, how do you feel?" she asks again. The worry is small, but it is there in the back of her voice.

"I'm fine, Ma." I breathe in the earthy smell of the tea. Some girls this age are just prone to fainting—that's what the doctors told us after the tests a while back. I'm supposed to take iron pills and stay hydrated.

"We need to go see Roger in the hospital," I say.

Ma looks at me, her head cocked. "Why on earth would we go see Roger?"

Granny is watching me closely. She reaches out and holds onto my wrist, sort of like she is taking my pulse.

"I think it's important," I stammer. The fact is, I really don't know why. I don't even want to go see him—I always get a funny, creepy feeling around him and my mouth always tastes of ash until he is gone. But I think about that packet of Lifesavers in my desk drawer that I will bring with me to the hospital, and I am determined.

"I don't think that's a good idea, honey. His Ma's probably there with him and I doubt she'd want to see us at the moment."

"Well, didn't she ask you to take Lucas for a while anyway? We can just meet there to pick him up."

She shakes her head. "No Len, no one's asked me to take Lucas."

"Well we need to go see Roger," I insist.

"We should listen," Granny says. "She woke up with the same look cousin Dweasel used to have when he'd had a vision."

"Not now Ma, please."

"Oh, these things are never convenient. It wasn't convenient when she insisted we call the vet in the middle of the night either, but if you hadn't done it you'd have lost both Bessie and her calf."

Ma is quiet. "We'll see," she says finally.

So I curl up with a book and rest as Ma suggests. It is early afternoon when the phone rings. When Ma hangs up, she comes into the room, her arms crossed in front of her.

"Okay, well Lucas is going to stay with us for a few days until Roger's Ma can handle things." She studies me, gauging my reaction. I try not to look too triumphant. "She's going to bring him over here day after tomorrow though. I don't want to meet her out somewhere."

My face falls.

"But I reckon if you really want to, we can go give our best wishes to Roger in the hospital," she goes on. "Surely no one can fault us for doing that. You can get your shoes on. We'll go when you're ready."

Before we leave, Ma checks to make sure the stock cows are out to pasture and the milking machine has been cleaned. We are quiet on the drive over, Granny in the front seat with Ma since she insisted on coming with us. The flat brown fields outside the window slowly give way to the suburbs and then the crushed together buildings of downtown.

I've been to the hospital only once before—the first time I fainted, and the school nurse thought it was a seizure and panicked. They kept me for hours and ran all these tests. I was eight and I remember Ma sitting beside me and reading to me—her theory was it was no good reading a novel because of all the interruptions—people always coming in to poke me with a needle or read the machines I was hooked up to. So she brought her worn out copy of Being and Time. Every nurse that came in gave us a double take, and finally I asked if she'd brought her anthology of poetry because I don't care how much she loves that stuff, Heidegger is not relaxing to listen to in a hospital bed with "The Young and the Restless" blaring from the next room, and the antiseptic smell and the machines beeping all around me. Give me "The Wasteland" any day over that.

We park and enter through the vast main lobby and are directed to Roger's room by the sour looking woman at the central information counter. We are quiet in the elevator. Finally, Ma breaks the silence.

"I don't know how Lucas is handling all this. We'll have to be very sensitive while he's with us."

She looks at Granny, not me, while she says this, and Granny widens her eyes and looks all innocent.

"Well of course we will," she says.

The elevator stops, and before the doors open, I pull the Lifesavers out of my pocket and hold out the package. Ma shakes her head, but Granny sticks her hand out right away, palm up. I put a green one on the palm of her hand and take a red one for myself, and when the elevator doors open, we both take a deep breath and plop the candies in our mouths.

CHAPTER 7

Len (2001)

There is a short walk, and we enter Roger's room cautiously. There is nothing special about it. It has a bed with a small table and armchair on one side and medical equipment on the other. Except for the TV mounted on the wall facing the bed, that is it. The TV is on, playing a daytime news show. No one else is there, just Uncle Roger, lying in the bed hooked up to an IV and sleeping—pretty much exactly as I saw him in my mind when I knew I needed to come here.

Ma hangs back a bit, but I walk right up to Roger's bedside. He looks smaller there somehow, thinner. He is pale, his face slack.

His breath is raspy, his lips dry and coated with white. There are long hairs growing right out from his nose, and I try not to look at those.

I close my eyes and hear the humming. It is soft and faint but it is there.

When I open my eyes I half expect a sign—a cross above the bed, the shadow of Mary Magdalene in the hospital sheets—something to show me there is a reason for my being here. But there is only the soft ticking of the machines and the noise of voices from the talk show on the TV where they are interviewing "emerging country music stars." Ma crosses over behind me to sit in the armchair, and she looks everywhere except at Roger. Granny stands beside me, reaches into her handbag, and making sure Ma isn't watching her, she pulls out a small rag tied up with a string.

It doesn't smell as bad as the one she placed under my back when I had pneumonia, or the one she left at Daddy Mo's house when he got the gout so bad he couldn't walk. That one almost made me double over and be sick right there. But this one has a soft smell—sort of like a wet dog in a warm kitchen. Granny reaches over the bedrail and gently places the ball underneath Roger's shoulder. She raises her eyebrows at me, winks, and pats my hand.

"OK then," she says. "Ready to go?"

I feel I must be missing something, but I reckon I must have just got it wrong. I thought I was supposed to come, but there is nothing for me here. I nod, disappointed, and turn toward the door.

Then, there is something in Granny's tone when she says, "Coralee?" Something that makes me turn back quickly to see what is wrong.

Ma is still sitting in the vinyl armchair, but she is staring at the TV screen, her face white, her mouth slack. She takes the remote control from the small table beside her and turns up the volume.

"Cora, what on earth?" Granny says, walking over to her.

But Ma puts her hand up like a stop sign and shakes her head, her eyes never leaving the screen. I have to walk back to Roger's bedside and turn around to face the door to see the TV, and when I do, there is some lady with big hair talking about the country music charts and interviewing a man wearing faded blue jeans and a cowboy hat. The caption underneath says: Clifton Wilkes.

Ma sits spellbound, as the man talks about his upcoming tour. I am hungry and tired, and I just wanted to go home, but there is something about that man's face that keeps me watching. There is something in his voice, and that humming sound is back in my head. It grows louder inside me so that I can't actually hear the words they are saying to each other, but I watch as the camera zooms in on Clifton's face and he flashes a smile. His eyes crinkle when he does, and his whole face lights up. I feel a little dizzy and I reach out and grab the railing on Roger's bed. Finally, the lady with big hair says goodbye to Clifton, and the show switches to people in suits sitting around the news studio. The humming in my head starts to recede and I am not so dizzy. Ma sits slumped a little in her seat like she's had the wind knocked out of her.

His face isn't on the screen anymore, but I keep thinking of Clifton Wilkes. Square jawline, brown eyes. He looks about like every other country singer I've ever seen, with his blue jeans and cowboy hat. But there is something else that I know in that moment—that I am absolutely sure of. Because I hear those whispers, even though there is no wind. And even without those, I would know. Because that man on the TV sure looks an awful lot like the man in the Polaroid in my drawer back home.

Suddenly there is a perky voice in the doorway. "Why hello there. Sorry to intrude on family time, I just need to check his vitals." The nurse marches in, her white tennis shoes squeaking, and picks up Roger's wrist. "The doctor's going to make rounds in about a half hour if you want to stay and talk to him." She smiles, chirpy and oblivious, and Ma stands up, shaking her head violently.

"Thank you, but we just wanted to come and give our best wishes. We've got to be going now."

She sounds like a robot, or like someone in those movies when an alien takes over their body or something, but the nurse just smiles and nods and makes a note on Roger's chart like nothing's wrong.

Before the nurse is done, we practically run out the door and onto the open elevator. None of us notice it is on its way up instead of down, and just when I open my mouth and say, "Alright Ma, are you going to tell me who that was on the TV?" the doors open and a nurse wheeling an empty wheelchair gets on with us.

Ma gives me a look that means she doesn't want to talk about it in front of the nurse. We travel down the fifteen floors in silence, Granny watching Ma out of the corner of her eye, and Ma staring straight ahead.

I follow them out of the elevator and out of the hospital and through the parking lot. But when we get to our car, I stand there, not opening the door. I look Ma right in the eye as she stands by the driver's side.

"That Clifton Wilkes—he's my daddy." I don't ask her, I just say it like the fact it is.

She looks away for a moment, looks back at me, opens her mouth, then closes it again. I cross my arms and stare at her. Finally, she shakes her head. "I don't think so, Len."

She looks deflated, tired, and she opens the door and gets in the car.

I get in the back seat and slam the door.

"Why were you looking at him like that then? Why does he look just exactly like the picture you gave me?"

She puts the car in gear and pretends to be completely absorbed with getting out of the parking lot. Granny sits beside her, watching her.

"I know it looked a little like him." Ma shakes her head. "But it wasn't him. I really don't think so."

I don't argue with her—for now I drop the subject. I just sit back, watching out the window, and I think about his face, that square jawline and that crinkly smile. I let Ma think about it too. Because no matter how much she wants to deny it, I know it was him.

CHAPTER 8

Jean (2001)

When it is time for me to meet with Jonny again, the huge metal door to the guard corridor clicks open. I hear slow, solid footsteps accompanied by a jangling of keys. The footsteps seem to go on forever. And suddenly, the guard is unlocking my cell and nodding at me to go with him. I stand, take a deep breath, and follow.

I am careful not to look into the other cells. Glancing in on private moments is a horrible feeling—I've walked by and seen nose picking, private itching and crazed muttering. But it is the silent ones that get to me. The empty eyes, staring vacant for so long—that is what I damn sure don't want to end up like.

I walk behind the guards, keeping my head straight. I picture them ladies from the PTA seeing me like this, and I let out a strange sound, in between a laugh and a choke. If they could only see me now, with their prim blouses and husbands in suits smelling of aftershave. They knew I wasn't one of them. They knew I hadn't grown up with my Mama being in the Junior League and hosting charity balls. But I was one of them enough to be in charge of the fund drive for new textbooks at the school. I was the one responsible, and getting the job done—at least at first. I don't even know what I did to mess it up. I remember, only dimly, waking fuzzy headed and groggy after one of the fundraisers. And after that, they wouldn't even talk to me. After that, when I went to the school and I saw those ladies, I would try not to look at them. I didn't want to see the way they stared. Sometimes it was with pity, sometimes with disgust, but I didn't want to see any of it. It must have been a doozy, whatever I done.

Jonny sits across from me. The room is empty except for the table between us and the chairs we sit in. He opens his briefcase, worn at the edges and scuffed, overloaded with bulging manila file folders. He pulls out a folder—not nearly as full as some of the others—and places it on the table beside his notepad.

"They tell me you wouldn't go to visitor's day."

I don't say anything. The truth is, I am aching for my baby boy. For the tousle-haired toddler who has turned into this sullen pre-teen, on the outside at least. My boy, who is my blood and soul, and who I know so much better than I know myself. But I can't face him yet. Not after what I've done to him.

"OK Jean," Jonny takes a breath and looks at me, his expression serious. "I need you to tell me what happened that night." He holds his pen ready, watching me.

I look down, squirm a little in my seat. I really don't want to talk about that night. I would rather stay in here for a good long time than have to talk about, or even think about that night.

"I don't know why…," I begin, my voice so quiet that even I can barely hear it.

"Don't worry about the 'why' right now," he says. "Look, this is my job—I do this all the time. You tell me what happened. My job is to figure out the best way to explain why it happened to the judge. Eventually to the jury, but first there's gonna be a preliminary hearing with just the judge. Start with that evening. You left the house to go out right?"

I nod. "I went to the game."

"Good," he says. "Let's start there. Tell me about that."

So I do. I tell him how Lucas had a baseball game, and he was going to spend the night at a friend's house afterwards. I had thought Roger was going to come too, but he didn't. He said he had some work to do to on the financials for the Claiborne job so that he could give them a bid. It was landscaping—his own business he started after getting laid off again.

So he stayed home and I left with Lucas for the game. Except that the other team never showed up. Some trouble with a broken-down bus we learned, and so they forfeited, and we all went home. I tell Jonny all about it, and I tell how, before Lucas got into the car with his friend Tom, I kissed him on the forehead and he rolled his eyes and pushed me away, embarrassed.

And then I left. I drove home and parked the car. I got out. I remember the sound my shoes made on the stone path from the driveway, and the different sound they made on the front steps. I remember turning the knob on the front door and thinking something felt wrong as soon as I opened it. I didn't know what, but something just didn't feel right.

I walked inside and closed the door behind me. There was soft music coming from the living room. Roger never played music when he was working. It's a weird feeling when something is not right in your home but you don't know what it is.

I take a deep breath. I don't want to go on. But Jonny nods at me, waiting.

"When I walked into the living room and I saw the candles on the mantel, I actually had a moment—a split second when I thought Roger had done it for me—the romantic atmosphere with music and candles. But then I saw them. They were over by the sofa so I didn't see them until I walked all the way into the room. And then there they were—Roger, and this woman, half dressed. I don't even really remember taking that gun out of my purse." I pause.

Jonny hands me a tissue and I take it just to have something to hold while I talk. "It was Roger's gun. He was getting the handle fixed on it, and I'd picked it up from Buck's earlier that afternoon for him. I just remember all of a sudden standing there and I had that gun in my hand and I was unlatching the safety."

I want to tell Jonny that I was surprised—that I could never have imagined Roger doing something like that. But the truth is, I was not. Because I knew for a long time that he didn't actually like me. I don't even know why he stayed with me when I think about it, because all I ever did was mess everything up.

But I was surprised she wasn't beautiful. I mean, maybe it sounds a little shallow at this point, but I reckon I was pretty insulted. I'd wondered before if he was having an affair. But in those moments, I'd pictured him being with a girl like in a magazine—someone I almost couldn't blame him for wanting to be with because she was so beautiful and so together. If she'd been like that, maybe I would have just started crying and not even thought about that gun that was just settin' there in my purse.

But she wasn't like those women in magazines. She was short with thick thighs and bad skin, and so I lifted that gun into the air. I didn't even really think about it—it felt like all the air was just being sucked right out of me.

And then I pointed that gun at him. Roger looked up at me with wide eyes and yelled, "Jean! No!"

I froze. My finger on the trigger. And then his face got red with anger. I could see it in his eyes, that look on his face when he was angry—I had seen it so many times over the years. He had that anger on his face and he started to talk. His lips started to curl up like they do when we are really fighting, and all he got out was, "What the hell --"

I didn't even let him finish his sentence. I just pulled the trigger, and there was the loudest noise I have ever heard in my life.

"Did you know ahead of time?" Jonny asks. "Did you know you'd come back to find him with someone?" He watches me closely as he speaks.

"No," I say.

"They're saying it was pre-meditated. That you came home early with a gun because you knew what you would find, and you planned to kill him."

My stomach does a flip at this. Dumb as it sounds, it never occurred to me that people might not believe me. I shake my head. "No. I picked that gun up at Buck's for Roger—I'd forgotten I even had it in my purse until I saw them."

He flips to a new page on his notepad. "Okay," he says. "Now, I want you to tell me about your relationship with Roger."

And so I do. I tell him about how we met and married, and how things started to get harder between us because of all my issues. It just all sort of gushes out of me—how I started to change, how I can't handle things the way I used to, how I was always messing up somehow. He listens and listens, and once in a while he asks a question. I go on a lot more than I mean to, and then I suddenly get self-conscious and stop talking.

He looks at me kindly. "Okay. You did great today, Jean. You really did. Now, don't worry or take this the wrong way or anything, but I'd like to bring in a psychiatrist to meet with you."

"You think I'm crazy?"

He shakes his head. "It's not that. It's something pretty routine in a case like this. I have to look at every angle to give you the best defense. I just want to bring her in to talk with you soon—you'll like her. She's really good."

"Well, I don't know," I say. "I doubt she's gonna like me too much." And when he starts to open his mouth to argue, I say, "Well go on then, you bring her on in to talk to me. There ain't much else I'm gonna be doin' to pass the time."

Later, back in my cell, I try not to think about that night. Funny, because so often I spend my time trying to remember things—where I put the car keys, what I said, what I did. And now—I am just trying to forget.

CHAPTER 9

Jean (2001)

The metal is cold against my forehead. I stand with my hands on the bars of my cell door, my head leaning against it. Someone down the hall coughs a harsh, phlegmy cough. Someone closer to me rocks back and forth on her cot in a rhythmic motion so we can all hear the gentle squeak of the springs. I try not to think about what she's doing.

I recognize the loud voice of the lady across from her when she shouts out, "Damn Girl!" That is it. No other commentary, but all across the massive room there are snippets of laughter and echoes, small and tinny, "damn girl!" People laugh. But the rocking goes on, no one cares.

It is almost lunch time. That's one of the "times" that matter around here. No one really cares what the hands of the clock say, except in relation to one of the "times." It is breakfast time and then exercise time and lunch time and shower time and social time and supper time and bed time. Those are the things that matter. And of course, "visiting time." I have promised to go to the next one of those.

The noises settle and still. I move over to my cot and lie down, the bent spring poking into my back. I close my eyes. I been visited quite a lot already. That baby face preacher stops by almost every day. And Jonny comes to tell me how Roger is still breathin' through machines and how he's still in a coma and they're not sure yet whether he's going to make it. Feels like I been here forever. Like the real kind of time—the time on the clock—means nothing. I go where they tell me and do what they tell me and don't talk to anybody if I can help it.

At twelve noon exactly we are let out for chow. I walk slowly down the block with the others. Without being told, we form two lines that snake all the way to the cafeteria. A sea of bright orange.

We shuffle in line. Slowly. From far away it would look so quiet. But if you got right down to our level, things are happening all over the place. The least movement closer to one of the other "girls" is a threat. Anything close to eye contact is a threat. I listen for anyone coughing or clearing their throat. I keep my eyes down, straight ahead of me. I am careful not to make any noise.

We get our trays. The five squares are already filled. I don't know why I had always pictured grumpy cafeteria ladies slopping food onto trays, but now that I'm here I know why that would never work. The girls in this place argue about everything. If someone got a larger serving than someone else, I can only imagine the fights that would break out. So the trays are pre-filled. Congealed baked beans in one square, red jello, corn sittin' in water, two slices of white bread, and some sort of round meat patty thing.

I slide my tray along the line; grab my carton of milk and plastic spoon, and shuffle over to the table to sit down. I learned the first day which corner to sit at. Next to nobody. Looking down at my food that I don't really want to eat. I push around the beans and take a bite. I pick up the meat patty thing and look at it closely.

"Wassa matta, Sugar?" Someone calls from the other side of the table. "You don't like seagull meat?" A bunch of other girls laugh with her. And then all of a sudden there is a form beside me, large and hulking. A bulky shape pulls back the chair beside me and sits down heavily.

It is Bonnie-Lynn, one of the old-school girls the guards always talk to friendly-like. She takes a moment to straighten her tray, then she looks at me, pursing her lips forward as if she is considering something. Bonnie-Lynn's hair is brown and long, and her face has acne which makes her look younger than she already looks.

"You a teacher or somethin' like that?" she asks, squinting at me sideways.

I shake my head.

"You read good though, right?" she asks. "I seen you reading before."

I try not to stare at her teeth that are so yellow in the front they are almost brown. I nod. "Yeah, sure," I say.

"Ever teach anybody?" she asks, narrowing her eyes at me.

"Just my son. When he was little—I helped him learn in kindergarten."

She nods. She turns to the other side of the table and says, "Ladies, you know what Sugar did to earn herself a spot in this here establishment?"

They shake their heads. One calls out, "She talk too loud in the library?" And they all laugh.

But Bonnie-Lynn says loudly, "She blew her old man away. Took one shot and she blew his head about clear off." They nod, silent and impressed.

She turns back to me. "What you want is the commissary." She says it with authority. "I wouldn't feed that seagull meat to my dog." And she spoons her beans onto her white bread, rolls it up like a jelly roll and takes a bite.

She chews, slowly and deliberately, watching me all the while. Then, suddenly, it is as if she has made a decision. She leans forward speaking low so the other girls can't hear. "I gotta get outta this place. I gotta file me an appeal." She pokes the corn on her tray with her spoon. "But my issue is that I ain't ever learned to read. We got this whole library in here, and everybody's goin' around being their own lawyer an shit— 'pro per' like they say. But how'm I supposed to file some dang appeal when I can't even read?" She leans back and nods her head at me as if she has just proved a point.

"I think we can make ourselves a deal. What you need in here is a friend—somebody to watch your back. What I need is a teacher." She leans back in her chair, assessing me.

I look at her, thinking about it.

"I don't know if I'm that great a teacher," I say. "Like I said, I only ever helped my boy learn and he had a real teacher at school anyway."

She shrugs. "Good enough for me," she says. "This afternoon, during free time. You meet me in the library."

I look down at my plate of runny, cold food. "OK," I say. I just can't picture things turning out very well for me if I say no.

Later, in the courtyard, I keep to myself. There is a track we are supposed to walk around, and some of the girls are playing basketball with a faded ball and a bald hoop with no net. No one bothers me as I walk around the track a couple times, then sit on the small bleacher area, the sun on my face. I keep to myself.

I used to get along with people. Not like I was Miss Popularity or anything, but in school, growing up, at my job, I always had friends. I never had to try so hard. I could talk with people and joke with them, easy-like. Without even thinking about it. Now it seems like no matter what, I end up saying the wrong thing.

It got so that Roger even tried to help sometimes—tried to help me think of things ahead of time to talk about with people. There was that Christmas party when we'd first moved into the neighborhood. We hadn't lived there long, and I wanted it to go well. He reminded me that Susan Olsen's mother had dementia, the Wycliffs just had a new baby girl recently, and Don and Franny Carmichael's son had just gotten accepted to TCU. So I was ready for small talk—it should have gone well.

I was nervous when we arrived, but after a while I started to relax. The big home on the corner was full of lights and a beautiful Christmas tree. There was a bowl of punch, and Christmas cookies, and I had on my sweater with sparkles and nice black pants. It felt good to be out of the house. It felt good to be around people. They were smiling and talking, and Roger left me to go talk to someone he saw on the other side of the room.

When I saw Don and Franny, I walked over and we clinked our glasses and said Merry Christmas. They asked about Lucas and I told them about how well he liked Little League and how hard he worked at school. I even remembered to congratulate them on the news about Don Jr. I don't know what else I said when I was talking to them, but after a while, Don and Franny muttered excuses and went off, leaving me alone. I went to the punch bowl. I saw the groups gathered and looking at me, whispering. I must have had another "moment"—something I didn't even remember, and I wondered what it was that had come out of my mouth.

I didn't even bother to try to talk to anyone else that night. I just stood in the corner drinking punch until I felt a little unsteady and Roger came to collect me. His face was hard, disappointed, on the way home. And when he suggested I take an aspirin so my head didn't hurt in the morning, I could hear the quiet sadness in his voice. He added, sort of softly like he was almost embarrassed to say it, "And Honey, you really should take a shower—I hate to say anything, but you smell pretty rank."

In the shower I felt frozen at first. It was hard for me to move. I was empty, like my insides had been scraped completely clean and I was just a shell. The water was warm and I turned it so hot it almost burned. I sank to my knees, letting it run over me. Maybe it would cleanse me. Maybe it would just finish me off. I didn't know who I was any more. I didn't know how I could possibly have lost myself so completely.

CHAPTER 10

Cora (1988)

Cora was the only one at the party whose T-shirt was held together with safety pins. It was not a party she would usually go to, but when Edison had asked, she somehow found herself saying yes. The friend he was staying with, Mike, was having people over—Mike and his roommate Roger with the Levi's and the creepy stare. Roger had asked her out once and ever since she had turned him down, she could feel the waves of animosity emanating from him.

She walked in a little wary. The apartment was packed with what looked at first to be a Frat boy crowd. Red solo cups were all around her. But over in the corner by the stereo, things looked a little better—a few guys with partially shaved heads, and a girl with pink hair and a pierced nose who was camped out by the stereo, apparently in charge of the music.

Cora saw Edison across the room and began to pick her way through the crowd. Near him she saw Roger with his arm around a girl with Wrangler's and feathered hair. The girl laughed adoringly as Roger spoke, and Cora was relieved. She caught Edison's eye, and his face suddenly brightened into a smile. There was none of the game-playing she was used to, the pretending not to care, the trying so hard to be cool, or at least cooler than the other. It was just a smile. It seemed so simple. She liked him – why should she pretend not to care?

She laughed when she saw her brother, Bo chatting up a blond. She caught his eye and smiled but she left him his space. Small town, she thought to herself. When she walked over to Edison, he kept talking to his friends, but he grabbed her hand, and held it, as if it were the most natural thing in the world. Not embarrassed in front of his friends, not pretending he didn't like her until he'd had a few more drinks. Just held her hand, warm and close and safe.

She felt that warmth the whole time she was at the party. They talked, and laughed, and danced until the neighbors called the cops and everyone had to go home. Edison drove, and his beat up Volkswagen bug started up the first time to their surprise. They drove past the city, they drove past the water tower, and he parked beside a field with a blanket of soft green grass, took her hand and led her to an area where a canopy of trees shielded them from the road.

It wasn't the first kiss that made her weak in the knees, it was the second. The first was a little unsure, a little tentative. But by the second kiss, she felt as if her whole body was fluid – she could not tell where she ended and he began.

It was all so easy, afterwards, and the next day. They spent as much time together as they could over the next few weeks. One afternoon she stayed at work an extra hour because the guy on shift after her was late. When she got to her house, she found Edison in the kitchen with her mother, aprons on, hands covered in flour, laughing.

"Your mom's teaching me how to make biscuits," he laughed as she walked in the room. They sat in the kitchen, eating warm biscuits and drinking cold milk, and when he kissed her, he left flour on her face.

Later that night, she lay on her back in the same field behind the farmhouse. She had said goodnight to Edison earlier, but she knew she wasn't ready for sleep. So she'd headed quietly out the back door and lay down to watch the stars. She would see him tomorrow night.

Cora could smell the sage in the warm night air. She heard the soft nostril-breath of the cows not far off and the quiet, steady munching as they grazed by moonlight. They did that sometimes in the summer—the heat sent the herd to the shade to sleep during the day, so they grazed by moonlight instead.

When you are in a Texas-sized field, smelling fresh grass, looking up at the moon, with the sound of cows munching quietly in the background, everything else can seem very far away. Cora found it hard to remember dorm rooms and professors, hard to care as much about those things that seemed as if they were from a different world. Somehow, she didn't need the tough attitude for these few moments at least. She felt raw—exposed and fragile.

There was a deep-inside part of her that was at home here in the house she'd grown up in, the fields where she'd spent countless hours as a child. But there was part of her that knew she never fit quite right in this town. Everywhere Cora went, she felt a little different from the pack. In her hometown, she was smarter and more worldly, at college, she was edgier and more rebellious, and with the party crowd she hung out with she was smarter and more ambitious. She felt she was pieced together from all these different sections, and nowhere did she feel completely whole, nowhere did she feel completely understood. Until now. It was like Edison somehow could reach inside and see and understand each of those pieces of her—like he appreciated all of her.

As she lay in the warm air in the moonlight, she smiled and felt as if the earth was reaching into her and giving her energy. She felt at one with everything she could see and sense around her. It was almost like she was high, but more quiet and even—she wondered if there would be a crash when she came down.

CHAPTER 11

Cora (1988)

They sat on the ledge of the water tower watching the sun sink down into purple. It was Tuesday—usually Cora would want to head to the Upstairs Lounge. But tonight, she didn't care whether they went or not. She looked at Edison's profile, took a small white pill out of her pocket and offered him half. "We can get more at the club if you want."

He shrugged. "I reckon I'm pretty happy just to sit up here for a while with you. We can go if you want though."

She tipped her head to the side, thoughtful. "Maybe later."

Her friends at Georgetown had laughed when she told them there was a decent club in Abilene. But there was—people came out of the woodwork from miles away to go to the Upstairs Lounge. Most other nights it was a different clientele, but on Tuesdays it was good. Maybe they'd go later, but she was in no rush. She realized that she had never actually been so content to sit on a water tower and not go anywhere or do anything.

They talked about movies, about books, about songs. They talked about truth, about hypocrisy, about art.

"I wrote you a song," he said out of the blue.

"Really?" It was the most romantic thing she had ever heard. "Sing it for me."

His voice was smooth, and she felt herself swoon inside just a little when he sang to her. His song was about love, and joy, and longing, and she had never heard anything so beautiful. It had an Elvis Costello feel, maybe a little of the longing of The Smiths. But it was unlike anything Cora had heard, and she knew in that moment, that she was not the only girl who would swoon hearing his voice. The thought made her protective, jealous, and she moved closer and put her head on his shoulder.

"It's all about the lyrics," he said. "Telling a story in as few words as possible, that's the challenge. When I listen to country music sometimes—I mean the good stuff like Johnny Cash, or the re-explored jazz/folk kind like Tom Waits—there's a story there even though they don't tell it all. Like poetry really."

Cora watched the moonlight where it touched his hair and listened.

Later, at the Upstairs Lounge, they felt the X coursing through their veins. Love in a pill. Everything was good, everything would stay like this forever. They drank, they danced, the music becoming their heartbeats, the world existing only so that the two of them could live in it together.

They came down slowly, sitting out on the fire escape as the sun rose pink in the sky, the Abilene air cool and dry. Later, Cora would remember this as the night before her world crashed into pieces. They sat talking, joked about getting married, about how many kids they would have.

Cora, still laughing turned to him and said, "But you haven't even told me you love me yet."

She didn't think about it before she said it. She never planned to utter the word "love." She was just talking. Just joking like they had been a moment before. As soon as it was out of her mouth she regretted it. But it couldn't be unsaid. She couldn't take it back or say she hadn't meant it. There was a flicker on his face. She didn't know what it meant, but she saw it. After what seemed like an eternity, he reached out his hand and cupped her cheek with his palm, his eyes never leaving hers, and said, "I love you."

"Really?" she couldn't help it, her face lit up like she'd won the lottery.

He nodded, smiling. "Really."

She couldn't say it back right away. Not until later, after they lay, spent, on the soft carpet of green grass and Cora knew she needed to get home before her mother woke. She said it then, softly, into his ear as he lay with his breath returning to normal. And as she did, she felt his arm tighten around her.

CHAPTER 12

Len (2001)

M a is quiet after our trip to the hospital. She goes to her room and shuts the door, not emerging even when it is supper time. Granny and I eat cold fried chicken and warm butter beans for supper, and then we sit out on the porch. The air around us is warm, and there's no wind. Granny rocks softly in her wicker rocking chair, her hands busy braiding long bits of pond reeds. One of the cows is due to go into labor any day now, and Granny swears that if she has pond reeds around her neck the birth will be easier. I sit on the porch swing and look out across the yard in the fading light. It is that time when the fireflies just begin to appear, and you wonder if they just came out because it was getting dark or if they've been there right in front of you the whole time and you just couldn't see them.

Something stops me from jumping right in and asking her about Clifton Wilkes. Instead, I ask, "Why do you think Aunt Jean shot Uncle Roger? I mean, I know what he was doing, and I get she'd be mad. But there's this thing called divorce, right? You can't just go around shooting people cause you're mad at them."

Granny looks at me and shakes her head. "Someday you'll fall in love Len, and then you might be able to understand your Aunt Jean. People fall in love in all different kinds of ways, and there just ain't no telling what it can do to you."

She puts the pond reeds in her lap and reaches out to smooth my hair. She looks out of the porch and past the barn. "The first boy I loved like that was Vernon Chaney. I was seventeen. He used to come help my daddy with branding the new calves."

She strokes my hair softly, still staring out into the distance. "Then I saw him at the spring dance, and I marveled at the way his snakeskin boots looked coming out of his jeans. When we danced he smelled like cigarettes and my heart fluttered. Then he took me behind the bleachers and I knew what it was supposed to feel like when someone kissed you. I guess I had kissed other boys before, but their hands on me always felt like they were thinking, 'I know I'm supposed to touch her here,' but they didn't really know why. Vernon knew why."

Granny looks down at me. "But that's not what I meant to be telling you about. I meant to be telling you about how people love." She sighs and looks away again. "You can love with your eyes or you can love with your belly. It's when you love with your belly that you have to watch out. It's the kind of love that when you look at the dark hair on your man's wrists, your stomach turns over and you see the whole world right there in his wrists and there's nothing else you want anywhere—that's when you need to be careful. When he treats you hard and you stick with him—that's when you gotta worry about yourself.

This is what I'm telling you Len—don't you ever let anyone take away that little piece of God inside of you, that part of you that you close your eyes and know is there. Sometimes they can take away your whole self and you don't even know it. They won't do it all at once. It'll just be that one morning you wake up and realize you've learned to love the pain in your gut, the wrenching, twisted feeling that comes from loving with your belly and him not loving you back. When you've lived with that twisting gut pain for so long, you can forget how to love unless that pain comes right along with it. That is the way your Aunt Jean got to, and that's why she did what she did."

This explanation makes no sense. I keep picturing Uncle Roger, with his big thick neck and fat face and hands, and it is inconceivable to me that anyone would love him enough to go crazy for him.

The moon rises as we talk, and the streaks of orange have all but disappeared. I look out across the blooming bougainvillea and the trellis overflowing with purple wisteria. My right foot touches the floorboards ever so slightly, just enough to keep a gentle swing going. Finally, I say what I have been thinking all evening.

"I don't care what Ma says, I know that Clifton Wilkes fella we saw on the TV is my daddy."

Granny stops rocking when I say it. "That's just what you said when you thought Mr. Sykes was your daddy. And Bobby Dines."

I shake my head firmly. "No, this is different."

And I am certain it is different. Because I loved Mr. Sykes, my fourth-grade teacher, and when I saw Bobby in his firefighter suit, walking so brave and tall, I was swept away. The photo I have is pretty old, and a little blurry, so in my defense, they really weren't such off-base conclusions. But I know that those were just wishes, as if I could make something real just by thinking it. I am older now, and I know this feeling isn't just a wish.

"I met him, you know," Granny says.

"You did?" Of course I didn't know. No one ever talks about it. "Well?" I ask. "Wasn't that exactly his face up there on the screen?"

Granny shakes her head. "I honestly don't know, honey. Sometimes they all look the same—with those cowboy hats on and all. I mean, it could be, but I just don't know."

We sit in silence for a while, Granny's fingers busy with more braids. I don't know what all the rest are for, but I know she will find a use for them. I don't say anything more about my daddy, but the more I think about it, the more certain I am. Granny is quiet. Every once in a while she nods and mutters to herself.

I know one person who won't think I am crazy—my Uncle Bo. And I smile to myself at my luck, because he is taking me hunting on Saturday.

CHAPTER 13

Len (2001)

I have a lot to think about as I tack up Cyclops. The morning air is crisp-cool and the moon is still out. I am in the barn earlier than usual, on account of Bo is coming to get me at five o'clock so we can get out to the blinds early. Walter hums as he works, pointing with his chin to the thick slice of banana bread wrapped in paper on his workbench.

I munch on it while I brush Cyclops. His coat has thinned in places. It will never be sleek and shiny like the other horses. His lower lip hangs down, sort of droopy like, below his upper lip. When he looks at me with his good eye, I kiss him on the muzzle and sneak him a corner of my banana bread. This is the horse I would choose over them all—I can trust him with my life.

As I ride out to the north corner, the song inside me is quiet. The moon is still out, but the sky in the east is tinged with orange and pink. I don't feel the heavy creep of darkness like sometimes, and the song doesn't rise up and need to get out. In that quiet, I have time to think.

Ma won't talk about my father. His absence has always been there, seeping around every corner of my life. Always, when I ask her about him, she clams up. She won't tell me what happened, or why he left, only that he left before either of them even knew I was on the way. But I wonder, sometimes, if that is the truth. I wonder if maybe he learned I was on the way and that was why he left.

Once when I was in first grade, I went over to my friend Marissa Haney's house. When her dad came home from work, her eyes lit up and it was like her whole world brightened—as if they had a secret world between them. He picked her up and swung her around in a hug while she laughed. And later, when he sat on the couch while we played with her dollhouse, she put down the toys, marched over to him with a grin, took his baseball cap off his head and turned it backwards. He let it sit there on his head, off kilter and silly, and he smiled at her. She was claiming him; he was hers. I made myself small and quiet as I watched them, pretending for a moment, that he was mine too—that I could walk over and feel the scratchy stubble on his face, and that he would tickle me while I squealed. And when he turned to me and smiled and said, "Hey there Len, how's your mama?" and put a hand on my head, I swallowed and fought back tears.

It was hard to get that echo out of my head—so many echoes, on the playground, at school—"this is my daddy," mine…mine. That confidence, that ownership, that something I could never have.

At the north corner, I turn as always and ride the western fence line back toward the barn. Rachel's house is in the distance, just off the paved road that winds on into town. Rachel and I have been best friends pretty much ever since she moved there two years ago. Her daddy isn't around much either—she's supposed to see him every other weekend, although it doesn't always happen—but at least she has one. And that right there is a world of difference.

I am itching to tell Rachel about Clifton Wilkes. But first, I am going to get to work on Uncle Bo. Because if anybody can talk to Ma about the whole situation, Bo can.

Dark orange streaks are just appearing in the sky when I come through the screen door to the kitchen, careful not to let it bang behind me. I wash my hands and mix tuna fish with pickle relish and extra mayonnaise, just the way Bo likes it. I always put lettuce on my sandwich and cut it in half, but Bo's I just wrap in plastic. He likes the feel of a whole, heavy sandwich in his hand.

Ma stumbles into the kitchen to make her coffee, looking like she has barely slept. She cocks her head to the side as she runs the water to avoid the African violet overflowing its basket.

"Did you get your lunch ready yet?"

I nod and point to the red and white cooler sitting beside the fridge.

"I want you to make sure you drink lots of water. You need to stay hydrated." She hands me a glass of cold water.

"Yeah—I got it."

"And promise me, if you start to feel funny or woozy, you just sit right down and tell Bo."

"Alright Ma."

"Because really what I worry about most is you knocking your head on something as you fall over."

"I'll sit down Ma, I promise."

Ma makes biscuits, I fry some eggs, and Bo shows up at 5:00 on the dot and sits down to breakfast with us. Bo reaches a large hand out—his two fingers nearly cover the saltshaker—and he covers his eggs with a layer of salt and pepper so thick I can see the granules, just sitting on top. I wince looking at it, but he digs in eagerly, scooping his eggs up onto his toast, and biting into the whole mound. He chews in wide, even bites.

I gaze at Bo's profile, his strong jaw line and straight nose, and think he looks almost like one of the men in the movies Ma liked to watch—the ones with the men in dark suits and their funny way of tipping their hats, and sometimes breaking out into song so that I get all embarrassed for them and can't even watch anymore. But then Uncle Bo stands up from the breakfast table, and I can see his belly, all set to burst out of his faded dungarees, and it's not quite like the movies anymore.

Ma holds me tight against her when she kisses me goodbye. "What bursting anguish tears my heart," she whispers as she cups my face in her hands, staring hard at me, squinting.

I roll my eyes at her quote. "I'll be fine Cora," I say.

"Don't call me Cora," she says to my back as I walk to the car. I ignore the look she exchanges with Bo.

Bo swings the cooler deftly into the back of his pickup where it sits below the gun rack. Harlan, his black lab, is back there too, lying on his chewed-up flannel pillow, a long line of drool hanging down from his tongue and landing on the rusty metal of the truck bed. I climb into the passenger seat. The handle for the window isn't in its socket, so I search the floor. Bo's pickup always smells of stale beer and ashes and a little foot odor. Somehow I find it very comforting, that smell. Bo flicks on the radio, turning the knob a hair so he can pick up the Stained-Glass Bluegrass hour.

I find the handle among the loose bits of paper, plastic bags, and other debris, stick it firmly in place and roll down the window. I close my eyes against the dust clouds until we get little ways to the paved road. Nothing but flat brownish green ahead of us except for the old farmhouse that sits in the corner of the field.

We drive on for another hour or so, talking here and there and watching the land unfold. The road follows Deerborn Creek which winds around north Abilene. Just past the park, we pull into a long private drive and stop under a tree. Bo grabs his camouflage shirt and binocular case out of the back of the pickup. He hands me the cooler, slings his knapsack over his shoulder, and takes the campstools in one hand and our shotguns in the other. He gives a whistle and Harlan hops out of the truck bed, mouth hanging open in excitement.

We make our way along a slim pathway beside the creek. It's about a half mile to the blind, and the air is still cool from the morning. The dry grass crunches beneath our feet. I have to stop myself from talking about what I want to talk about. I have to wait for the right time to bring it up. I think of the Indians. I try to walk flatfooted like them and silent. I try to be like a man with a shotgun, strong and unafraid. I picture my daddy here, ahead of Bo, leading us onward and telling us about the different plants, the prints of animals in the mud, and the scents in the wind. He would know about all of that, I am certain.

As we walk, there is a charm I say under my breath, and I send it in waves out all around us. It is one that Granny gave me long ago, and I say it now for the ducks, because I love everything about these hunting trips—the early mornings, Harlan's slobbery panting, the clean metal smell of Uncle Bo cleaning his shotgun—but I know for certain that I never want to shoot a living thing.

The blind rises suddenly beside the path, a dark wooden structure inside a forked tree and covered with leaves and branches. We climb the steps stuck in the thick trunk, Bo hoisting his gear ahead of him so that it falls heavily onto the wooden floor. We set up our campstools and sit down to wait.

Bo can sit still for hours. It used to unnerve me how still he could sit. I'm used to seeing him wielding a hammer or carrying two-by-fours, always doing something. But when he is in that blind, his gun against his knee, and his head cocked slightly like a puppy, Bo can sit still as a fence post for hours on end. The only things that break his repose are sips of coffee from the thermos top beside him or a sound from outside. Then he will lift his gun so smoothly it is like another one of his limbs, aim, steady and strong, and shoot. It happens in one fluid motion, like a dance—it is beautiful even. As beautiful as a beer-gutted man with a red face and a shotgun can be, I reckon.

We sit, stock-still and quiet for most of the morning. I let the breath become a rhythm—once it does that you can see things in your head without even closing your eyes.

We reach that moment, where just being is enough. Where we are there together but each alone looking out at the world. And that is when I think—it is time.

"Uncle Bo," I say softly, like waking someone up.

"Hm?" he says it like a question, still staring out the window.

I hesitate. Once I say it, once it is out in the open, I won't be able to take it back. And in a strange way, sometimes it feels better to have the hope, better to have it be a question. Because who knows what the answer to that question is gonna be. I take a deep breath.

"You ever heard of Clifton Wilkes?" I watch Bo closely, but there is no jolt of recognition on his face. "He's this country singer. I saw him on a talk show on the TV."

Bo shakes his head, his eyes still staring out of the blind. "Nope. Never heard of him."

"Well, I saw him on the TV," I repeat. "Ma saw him too. She went white as a sheet, and she had to sit down and everything. And now she won't even talk about it."

He turns to me then, his face a question.

"I think it's him," I say. "I think he's my daddy."

Bo shakes his head, his face sad. "Len, I know it's hard your mama won't talk about him—"

"But you should have seen Ma," I insist. "All those singers, they never go by their real names anyway. He was talking about his concert tour. Ma just sat down and she almost started shaking, I swear. And he looks just exactly like the picture I have."

"Len, that picture was taken over twelve years ago. I bet the guy has changed an awful lot since then. Plus, it's so fuzzy you can barely make him out. It don't tell you squat about what he'd look like now."

We sit for a while, quiet, and I can tell he is thinking about it. Finally, he nods almost to himself. "Well, I'll talk to her. But you know even I can't get her to talk about that topic."

I smile, a small bit of relief washing over me. My heart is racing a little—if Bo can talk to her, maybe, just maybe, she will admit that it's true. It is a lot to hope for, I know. But still I smile to myself even as I send out a little song into the wind, telling those ducks to just stay put—telling them whatever you do, do not fly away.

CHAPTER 14

Jean (2001)

We move along, out of our cells and toward the showers—not all the inmates at once. Our group is about twenty. I follow the other girls. I keep my head down and I do what they do. It is not like you see in the movies—I was worried about that the first time. Here there are private stalls with curtains, the guard hands us each a towel and we get two minutes of hot water. Those two minutes are pure bliss.

When I come out from behind my curtain, I am fully dressed and still towel drying my hair. None of the girls mess with me. But one of the guards stands right outside staring. I keep my eyes down and gather up my things.

I'm not scared. Even if no one else was around and he tried something I don't reckon I'd be scared. I am a master at detaching from my body. I understand how to just leave and not care what is happening to the flesh and bone and skin that is lying there below me. I been doing it for years, whenever Roger wanted me. Trying to feel something —— something like I used to feel when we first were dating, back when things were sweet and I would get a little thrill when he touched me. I don't remember when things changed—maybe it was after Lucas was born because I was so tired after holding the baby all day, I just wanted my body to myself. Most times I just desperately wanted him to get off of me—stop smothering me, pushing himself onto me and into me. I'd hold his prick in my hand and I'd imagine squeezing so hard it would burst apart, and there'd be nothing he could push into me anymore.

I know that is not normal.

I know that means there is something wrong with me.

He never had any idea about that. He'd just wonder how I could be so cold, like an ice queen—how I could never want him when I was his wife and I was supposed to love him. He'd be so hurt if I said I was too tired. So hurt that he'd want to keep talking about it and talking about it and in the end we'd end up doing it anyway. So I learned to just cut to the chase and do it even when I was so tired I just wanted to cry.

I got real good at pretending. I got good at never saying no. But underneath, it was like I was barely there. I put myself away, way back in a drawer somewhere, and just put on the face that smiled and said yes. I wore that self for so long I'd even forget that I had another self tucked away somewhere.

It is almost visiting time, so instead of going back to my cell, the guard leads me to a large room. It has booths in the middle, facing a wall of Plexiglas and booths on the other side. At one of those is Ma, with Lucas sitting beside her. His hair is slicked back and he's wearing a starched plaid shirt with a collar. He'd have hated having to dress up like that. He'd have hated Ma taking a wet comb to his hair. And I know without even seeing his face, how much he doesn't want to be here. He would feel that way even if his daddy wasn't in the hospital knockin' on death's door. And right now, I am certain that he hates me worse than he's ever hated anybody his whole life.

I sit down in the metal chair and face the clear plastic barrier. I face my mama. She purses her lips together tight and shakes her head just a little like she doesn't know what to say. I don't know what to say either, and then I realize I am pursing my lips together too, just like her.

"Thanks for coming, Ma," I say finally.

Her face softens just a little.

"They say Roger's stabilized," she says, raising her eyebrows and shrugging so I know she doesn't have any information other than that word that don't mean much of anything at all.

I nod, looking only at her. I can't bring myself to look at my boy. I can't bring myself to look into his eyes that are so much like Roger's and see the hurt and confusion that I have brought to him.

"Is he stayin' in school?" I ask, nodding over toward Lucas.

Ma glances over at him. He's facing forward, on purpose not looking at me. But I know he can hear me.

"Mostly," Ma says. She looks old. Older than when I saw her last. I try to remember how long it has been. We live maybe fifteen minutes away from each other, but I started seeing less and less of her over the years.

"How you holdin' up?" she asks, her eyes darting over my bright orange jumpsuit.

"I'm alright," I say, watching Lucas. I want to reach out my hand to him—ruffle his hair as if he were a toddler again.

Our time is not up yet. But I have nothing else to say. "Thanks for coming, Ma," I say again. I stand up, hesitant, and turn to Lucas. "I know you're mad, honey. I don't even know what to say to you about everything. But I love you Boo. I want you to know that, no matter what happens."

He doesn't move, just bites his lip, and I realize, this is the first moment I have actually wanted to leave this place.

I turn away and the guard walks with me to the door and out of the room, down the long corridor back to my cell. There is time before dinner, and I lie down on my cot. I'm supposed to see that psychiatrist tomorrow. Maybe she can sort it out. I figure it is about time someone other than Roger finally said it out loud that I'm crazy.

I tried to hide it, and so did Roger. There was that night when his friend, Boyd, came over for dinner. We sat talking and eating and I felt I was doing just fine. But then, I got up from the dinner table when Lucas called to me from the other room—and when I came back to the table, my chicken fried steak was more than half gone, and my potatoes almost finished. I stared in confusion.

"What's the matter?" Roger asked.

"I only took about two bites of my dinner before I got up." It was not the first time this had happened, but it was the first time anyone other than Roger had seen it.

"Oh honey," he said, real calm, "let's not do this now, ok?" He tilted his head just slightly at Boyd. It didn't look good for me to show my crazy in front of his friend, when here we were having a nice dinner and everything seemed normal.

So I just smiled and shook my head. And we went on with dinner and I didn't mention that I also didn't remember drinking half the beer in front of me. I thought I only took one sip. Boyd was talking and laughing with Roger—it all seemed so normal. I knew it then. There was definitely something wrong with me. There was no doubt about it that time.

That's when I decided to see a doctor. Not a psychiatrist—I wasn't willing to try that yet. I thought maybe it was something medical. So I made an appointment for a couple weeks later.

I walked into the doctor's office and gave my name to the receptionist. I was nervous and biting on my lower lip.

The receptionist checked her book, wrinkled her forehead and then flipped a page.

She looked at me, trying to smile politely.

"I'm sorry," she said. "We have you down for tomorrow."

"What?" I said. "I specifically made the appointment for today, I'm sure I did."

She pursed her lips, looking down at her book. "Well, you originally set it for today, but it looks like then you rescheduled it."

I shook my head. "There must me some mistake. I never rescheduled."

She put a pink fingernail next to a note in her calendar and read out loud, "Patient rescheduled to July 15."

I was shaken. I didn't remember calling, but of course, that's why I was there wasn't it? "Is there any way you can squeeze me in today?" I asked. "It's going to be much more difficult for me to come back tomorrow—I'll need to find a sitter for my son."

She shook her head. "Sorry, the doctor is completely booked for this afternoon."

I sighed. I said okay, but I dreaded facing Roger.

"Are you kidding me?" he said when I told him. "I took time off of work today to look after Lucas so you could go!"

"I'm sorry Roger," I said. "I don't understand it. I don't remember calling—I don't know why I would."

He was quiet, but I could see that anger, that exasperation just below, in the way he held himself still.

"I don't even remember calling to reschedule. It doesn't make any sense, I don't know why I would do that."

And so on the day of the appointment, we dropped Lucas at a friend's house, and Roger came with me to the visit to make sure I didn't get confused.

CHAPTER 15

Len (2001)

B o swings the screen door open wide and throws his arms up in the air—his way of showing we shot no ducks today. Ma smiles and glances at me. She is "philosophically opposed" to hunting, but always lets me go because she wants me to have a "strong male influence" in my life.

I wash up, the bathroom sink turning brown with all the dust coming off my hands. And when I come out of the bathroom, I hear them talking in the kitchen. Bo is typing on the computer.

"Look Cora," he says. "That's him. You know it is."

I stand outside the doorway, trying not to breathe.

"No I don't. It's been a long time—he looks old—I can't tell for sure."

"It's him Cora—Jeez, I can see that much and I only met the guy a few times."

My heart is beating so loudly I fear it will give me away. But I stand, frozen, waiting.

"What happened anyway?" Bo's tone goes softer, more cajoling. "You wouldn't talk about it then, I get that. But it's been a long time now."

"I don't think talking about it is going to do anyone any good." Her voice sounds tired. "I was stupid, OK? I was a stupid, gullible young girl, and I made a terrible mistake, OK? That's all there is to say about it."

It suddenly feels like I've just gotten the wind knocked out of me. To hear her come right out and say I was a mistake is like a punch to the gut. I sink down with my back against the wall and curl into a ball. I am not crying, I'm just quiet. For some reason, I am thinking of Roger. My hands ball into fists in hatred, although I can't imagine what any of this could have to do with him. Maybe if we hadn't gone to the hospital to see him, I wouldn't ever have heard her say that.

"Len! What on earth?" Granny rounds the corner and sees me. Ma and Bo are suddenly at the doorway, and I stand up quick.

"I'm fine," I say, working hard to make my voice normal. "I'm hungry," I add to get them off my case. Ma hands me a biscuit, still warm from the oven and makes me sit down. Granny feels my forehead, but I shake her off.

"Your cheeks are flushed—do you feel lightheaded?" Ma asks.

"No." I can't quite keep the anger out of my voice. "I'm fine Cora."

"Don't call me Cora," she says.

She makes me lie down anyway. So I lie on my bed, with a book in my hands, but I can't read. I just keep thinking about what she said. If I was that big a mistake, maybe it's no wonder my daddy left before I even got here. Ma comes in and sits on the end of my bed. I don't make it easy for her to talk. I pretend she isn't there and keep right on looking at my book.

She opens her mouth a couple of times but closes it up again before anything comes out. Finally, she looks defeated.

"You want to go over to Rachel's this afternoon?" she asks. "Maybe you girls want to head out to the pool for a bit?"

"Maybe," I shrug, but I don't look up from my book. I know I will be going to Rachel's, because before I overhead Ma, I was itching to tell her about who my daddy is. I haven't quite decided yet whether I'm going to tell her about what I just heard.

She pats my leg and stands to leave. My stomach tightens, but I stop myself from calling out to her as she leaves the room.

CHAPTER 16

Len (2001)

After lunch I grab my bag for the pool and my flip flops. Ma is sitting at the kitchen table with a stack of bills and her checkbook, and Granny is at the stove stirring a pot with a dark, bubbling liquid.

"I'm going over to Rachel's," I say, taking the sunscreen out of the cabinet and putting it in my bag.

"Okay," Ma says. "Just make sure—"

"I know Ma—I'll drink water and I'll sit down if I feel dizzy." Under my breath I mutter, "Why do you care anyway?"

Ma looks at me sharply. "What did you say?"

"Nothing."

"Len," she takes a deep breath, "I know you think...."

I stand there, by the screen door, looking impatient.

"I mean, none of this is simple."

I nod, my hand on the door handle.

Granny watches us. "I don't know about that Rachel," she says. "I'm not sure she's the best influence."

"You're calling someone else a bad influence?" Ma's eyes widen in disbelief and she shakes her head. Granny shrugs as if she has no idea what Ma is talking about, and in spite of the sadness in the pit of my stomach I almost smile at them.

I pull open the screen door, and just then I see Cisley's car pulling up into the drive.

"Oh." Ma looks at the clock. "I can't believe I forgot—that'll be Lucas." She comes out the screen door and stands beside me.

Cisley shimmies herself out of the driver's seat. She wears jeans with rhinestones covering the back pockets, and it is clear she's found time to go to the salon because her nails are a matching sparkly silver.

The passenger door opens slowly, and my cousin steps out. Lucas is a year younger than me, but you would never have thought it. He is tall and thick. His hair is cropped close to his head, military style, like his dad's. His face is round and freckled. I know that he's strong as heck, 'cause I've seen him wrestling with Dan Eubanks, who's a full year older and big for his age. But somehow, in spite of his bulk, Lucas looks soft when you see him. I can't help but feel a little sorry for him, standing all alone and staring up at our house.

He walks slowly in Cisley's wake. I make myself stand beside Ma even though I am itching to head out, digging the toe of my flip flops into the soft earth on the footpath. I smell the thick wave of Cisley's perfume before she reaches me. I think of that pink spray they sell at the dollar store that mostly smells like baby powder. The one that says "If You Like Armani, Then You'll Love 'Armano''

She sighs dramatically and makes a sad face. Her eyelashes are the same sleeping spiders that have scared me ever since I can remember—that along with her face being a different color entirely from her neck. She puts her arm around Lucas, and even though it all seems overdone, I see up close that her eyes are red, and she truly does look close to crying.

"Thanks for taking him, Cora. You know I'd do it if I could, but with those pills the doctor gave me for all this stress, I just can't manage."

"It's no problem," Ma says, reaching out to ruffle Lucas's hair as if he is still a little kid. I stand awkwardly, not sure what to say.

Lucas turns to me. "Hey," he says, almost normal.

"Hey," I reply, just as if his Ma weren't sittin' in prison. And suddenly, as much as I need to talk to Rachel about my Daddy, and what Ma said, as much as I am about to burst with holding all that inside of me, I also want to stay and hear what Lucas has to say. But he glances down at the striped bag I am carrying with a beach towel stuffed inside. "I was just fixin to head over to my friend's house," I say. "We're probably gonna go to the pool—you wanna come?"

He shakes his head. "Na."

"There's a high dive," I say.

He just looks down at his feet. I feel guilty for carrying on like things are normal—cause here he is basically an orphan. Here I am thinking my situation is so terrible and all, but when I think about Lucas, there ain't and no way around it that his situation is worse than mine.

We all stand there, awkward for a minute. "Are you hungry?" Ma asks. "I can fix you some lunch."

Lucas shakes his head. "I'm good." He holds a large duffle bag. "I brought my PlayStation. Can I set it up?"

Ma looks relieved. "Absolutely," she says. "You know where the TV is, you go right ahead."

He nods and heads on down the hall to the living room.

I can almost see the big cloud of sadness that surrounds him as he walks down the hallway. It shimmers slightly around the edges and grows and retracts with his breathing. I know somewhere deep inside that even the song inside me is not going to improve my cousin's situation. And he is sure not gonna want to talk to me while he is playing Grand Theft Auto or whatever. Plus, I have this feeling that if I stick around much longer, I am not going to be able to hold everything in anymore. So I say bye to Ma and get going.

The road is so hot it sends shimmers into the air. I walk along the side, the dust and gravel kicking into my toes when I drag my flip flops. My father's name is Clifton Wilkes. And even though I know that is a stage name, I can still pretend that makes my real name Lenora Wilkes, not Lenora Walker like I have been so far my whole life. I am different somehow, without anything else even happening. I feel more sure-footed, more balanced over the earth than I have ever been before. Because Ma can deny it all she wants to, but I know it is him.

I picture my daddy reading the letter I'm gonna write— maybe he'd just be getting ready to go on stage when he opens the envelope. Then he'd rush out of the stadium, leaving his fans and his manager and everyone in shock, and drive all the way here from wherever he is, with tears streaming down his face at the thought that he missed all those years of me growing up.

There is no shade on this stretch of road, and the sun beats down on me so that by the time I make it all the way to Rachel's driveway, small beads of sweat are rolling down the sides of my face and my throat is dry. And even though my feet are more firmly on the ground, something is still off-kilter. I am still off-balance, still stung from Ma calling me a mistake.

There are three stone steps leading up to the porch, and a mat in front of the door saying "Our home is your home." I reach over and ring the doorbell.

After a moment the door opens and Rachel's mom appears, heavy and slow, her hair even more unkempt than usual.

"Hi sweetie," she says. "Come on in—Rachel's just upstairs." She turns her head toward the staircase.

"Rachel, Len's here!" she hollers.

It happens rarely, but there are some moments I can see a person in my head. Sometimes it's a flash, like a photograph, and sometimes it's just a feeling or even a color. Usually when it happens it is with some random stranger who shakes my hand or pats me on the back and I get a jolt, like a tiny lightning bolt. Mrs. Corbin is not a stranger—I can't even count the number of times I've been near her before. But I've never seen her before with those dark circles under her eyes. And as I walk through the doorway, she pats me on the shoulder, a gentle, soothing pat, and it is as if a huge gust of wind reaches right inside me. Then it's like a movie screen right before my eyes. I see a little girl with bare feet sitting on porch steps as a car drives away, a brown leather belt snapped so that it makes a cracking sound, a room with a concrete floor and a bare, dirty mattress. And then the wind suddenly leaves me and I am sucking air, leaning against the doorframe to steady myself.

"Oh, are you all right, hon?" Mrs. Corbin asks.

"I'm fine," I say quickly.

Mrs. Corbin furrows her brows but turns away. Her slippers flap on the wood floor as she walks back to the kitchen where the TV is blaring.

The old farmhouse has faded wood floors, and the paint on the ceiling is peeling. There is not a space anywhere that isn't a complete mess, but by now, I know how to navigate my way around it. In the living room, magazines, newspapers, pairs of eyeglasses and half-filled coffee cups cover every table. The sofa is strewn with clothing, and piled onto the cushions are stacks of blankets, dishtowels, and other linens. In between the furniture are piles of junk—waist-high stacks of old magazines and books, boxes with random items piled on top of them—a coffee pot, a candle, old batteries. But through every room there is a sort of walkway. I've learned to just follow the trail. I make my way through the living room and up the stairway. As I step into Rachel's room, I breathe a sigh of relief.

Here, there is order. Light pink walls, white lace curtains with matching bedspread, a bedside table with nothing but a lamp and a clock on it. The plastic horses Rachel insists she is too old for but never seems to be able to part with are placed at exactly the same angle facing outwards on a single shelf of her bookshelf. And the bottom shelf holds books standing precisely in order of height.

Rachel sits at a small vanity table in front of a mirror making kissing faces. "Which side of my face do you think is best?" she asks, turning her head from side to side while keeping her eyes on her reflection in the mirror.

"I don't know," I shrug. "They're both pretty good I guess." But I know, even as I say it, that it is an understatement. Rachel has the sleekest dark hair, the bluest eyes and the poutiest lips I have ever seen, except in a magazine. There is no way around it, she is honest to goodness just beautiful.

"Dove soap is having this contest. You have to make a videotape—you just introduce yourself and say what town you're from—and then you send it in and if you win you get to be in one of their TV commercials."

"I bet you'd win, Rach," I say. I mean it too. And I am trying to be patient.

"I don't know," she seems deflated for a moment. "It's probably a stupid idea. I think what they really want is a mother-daughter duo—that's how they made it sound anyway. So you know that's not gonna happen." She turns away from the mirror toward me and shrugs. "How am I ever gonna get an audition like the one I need living all the way out here in the sticks? I need to get to Dallas, that's what I need to do."

I drop my bag by the door and sit on the bed, making a slight indentation on the pristine white quilt. "Rach, I've got news."

Rachel turns to me, serious suddenly. She can hear it in my voice, I am sure. "What's up?"

So I tell her. I tell her all about my vision of Roger in the hospital bed, about the TV show with Clifton Wilkes, and about how I am certain it is really him.

Rachel's eyes are big. "Wow," she says as she takes it all in.

I nod. "Yeah," I say.

"So, what's his music sound like?" Rachel asks.

I realize suddenly, that all this time I have been thinking about him and focused on getting the truth out of Ma, I haven't even thought about what his music sounds like. I shake my head. "I don't know. They played something on the show, but I wasn't really paying attention to that part of it."

"We should go to the mall—I bet they have an album of his at Sam Goody."

I nod. It's a good idea.

Rachel turns back to the mirror. "We'll have to take the bus—my mom's not having a good day." She makes her eyes big in the mirror as she brushes her hair, then runs lip gloss over her lips and smacks them together. She grabs a purse from a hook on the closet door, and pauses, looking thoughtful. "I bet your dad's got connections. I bet he could help me get a good break."

I shrug. "Yeah, maybe." Best not to ruin Rachel's mood by pointing out the challenges that plan entails.

CHAPTER 17

Cora (2001)

Cora zooms in so that the picture of Clifton Wilke's face fills her entire computer screen. She is calmer now and can look at it without feeling the bottom has dropped out from underneath her feet. At the hospital in Roger's room, what she had noticed first had been his voice—not just his voice, but the song he sang. He had sung it for her all those years ago. When she had thought she was special. When she thought he had written it for her. Before, apparently, he had taken a stage name.

But now, after the initial shock, she examines the face on her computer screen. It is different then she remembered— aged of course, filled out a little—but most of the difference is just from thirteen years of not seeing him, but picturing him. Somehow after all that time, the picture she had in her head didn't exactly match the reality. But as she looks closely, as she pulls up other pictures of him, album covers, promotions, and the like, the cogs of memory shift and began to align with what is in front of her. She feels the familiar ache, the deflated feeling in her chest that still, after all these years, comes to her anytime she thinks of that night he left.

She's recalled that moment, that phone call, so many times over the years that every detail is etched in her memory. Her casual excitement when she dialed his number to make plans for the evening. Roger's voice on the line telling her Edison had gotten a call from his agent and had packed up and headed to Dallas for an audition. No, he hadn't left any message for her, no he hadn't left a phone number or anything.

Cora had hung up the phone, then sat there staring dully at it. Maybe Edison was going to this thing in Dallas and then coming back. Of course he'd call her. He was just in a rush, and he'd known she wasn't at home. That's what Roger had said on the phone wasn't it? That he'd gotten a call from his agent and had to leave town right away. He just didn't have time to reach her. He'll call, she told herself. She sat on her childhood bedspread, hugging her knees to her chest.

But. She remembered his hesitation the night before, and she kicked herself for blurting out what she'd been thinking. Of course it would scare him away—he'd known her a few lousy weeks and she was already asking if he loved her? Already talking about their future? Jesus, what was wrong with her? But deep inside, she hadn't felt it was wrong. She'd known, with absolute certainty, what she felt for him. She'd known that the electric shock feeling of fitting so perfectly with another person did not come around very often, and she'd known that she loved him with every piece of her heart.

But. She had just assumed he felt the same way, hadn't she? What if she was wrong and he was just a player? What if it was an earth-shattering lightning bolt for her, but for him it was just another notch in his belt? She couldn't believe that. But then again, isn't that exactly what someone who's a player does—work to make them all believe the fairy tale? Well, she would know for sure soon enough. He would call her. She was certain he would. It was silly to think he wouldn't, really. She just needed to relax and do something else for a while, and he would call.

So she went to work, came home and helped Ma with the cows. Read some Husserl. Called Tessa, careful not to mention Edison or anything related. Late that night she reminded herself that he would be busy. He'd had to race to Dallas for whatever the gig was, and he wouldn't have a chance to call, and he knew not to call late because she was at her mom's house. She knew all that, but it did not help her fall asleep.

At the end of the next day she lay in bed. Could it really be that Edison had simply taken off now that he'd gotten what he'd wanted from her? She'd never thought of sex like that before. It seemed so cliché, it was hardly possible. But there it was, the cold hard, clichéd fact spread out before her—he'd pursued her until she'd slept with him, and then when it was clear she was getting serious, he'd gotten the hell out of Dodge. She'd always been so tough. She'd always been so guarded with her feelings. But there it was. It felt like she'd been punched in the gut so hard she could barely breathe.

Cora lay in bed remembering the feel of his skin, the way their bodies entwined so easily together, that feeling of connection, the peace she felt when she was with him. She had never before felt so completely understood and unconditionally loved. The thought that he must not have felt it too—that to him, she must have been just another girl, made her actually nauseous. It made her question her entire sense of reality. Perception—this was what she studied in her philosophy courses—this is what, academically, she found so interesting. How could her experience have differed so dramatically from his? And how could she ever make sense of the world and of life if she could not trust her own perception of reality? It was not just theoretical. It was everything to her.

She pictured him driving to Dallas, the window rolled down and the radio on. She pictured him telling his friends about the girl he'd scored with in Abilene, maybe laughing as he told them. He would tell them that she used the "L" word, and that he knew that was his cue to pack up and get the hell out. She forced herself to imagine it, to get herself used to the idea that he was not the person she had thought he was. She curled up in a ball and closed her eyes, willing herself not to cry.

There is no doubt, as she looks at his face on her computer screen now, almost fourteen years later. It is him. Cora doesn't want to admit it, but there is no doubt. She sits for some time pondering her next move. Of course, the internet doesn't provide her with contact information—the closest thing she can find is an address for the Clifton Wilkes Fan Club. This is definitely not going to be easy. She thinks about it a long time. Finally, she begins to write.

She writes the letter first, longhand and in cursive. She writes an email too, but she can't quite bring herself to hit the 'send' button. The letter though, she forces herself to put a stamp on and drop in the mailbox. After she posts it, she knows it would be absurd to expect a reply. She knows that, even though she's written "to be delivered personally to Clifton Wilkes" on the outside, that it will not be, and that the head of the fan club (she pictures a peppy high schooler with a skirt and cowboy boots) will laugh off her letter as some crazy stalker type. She had wanted to write his real name on the envelope—or at least inside—to give her some credibility. But, it would seem odd, wouldn't it, to claim to have had a child with someone and then not even know their last name. Of course it was odd. Ridiculous really. But all the same, she started her letter with "Dear Edison."

And all the same, after she drops it in the mail, she waits every day with anticipation for the mailman to arrive. She knows she will not get a response, but still she holds her breath every time she opens the mailbox, and lets it out in disappointment after searching through its contents.

CHAPTER 18

Jean (2001)

I meet Bonnie-Lynn in the library, and we find a small table in the back. I don't have much idea what I'm gonna do to teach her. I figure I'll start just like Lucas did in preschool, learning the names and sounds of the letters. For that, we mostly need a pencil and paper, not books. But they have plenty of each in the library, and Bonnie-Lynn insists we put a few legal books on our table so if anyone asks she can tell them we are working on her appeal. That is what I am supposed to tell anyone who wants to know.

So we sit, surrounded by books with long, impressive names, stacked up three and four high. And in the middle of all that, I write the first ten letters of the alphabet clearly on a piece of paper. I have Bonnie-Lynn repeat the name and the sound over and over again until she rolls her eyes at me. Then I write the next ten letters and we do the same thing. Bonnie-Lynn is not dumb. She does not have a razor-sharp memory, but she is not dumb. And within the afternoon she knows the sounds for two thirds of the letters. I think that's pretty good progress for one day.

"So when do I get to read?" she asks, a little exasperated.

"Well, this is like the first step," I say. "Once you know all the sounds, then you look at the word you want to read, and you just say the sounds out loud in order."

She looks at me a little skeptical. "That's it?"

I nod. "Pretty much," I say. "I mean, it's not that easy because when you put the letters together, they don't always have the same sound as when they're apart. But that's pretty much the concept."

"Huh." The corners of her mouth turn down like she is really thinking about this. Then she says, out of the blue, "I got a daughter."

I raise my eyebrows. "Yeah?"

She nods. "She was two years old when I came in here. Didn't get to see her learn to read." She is quiet for a moment. "She's eight now. She'll be twenty-four when I get outta here. Won't even know me."

I remember when I used to help Lucas. In those sweet early days when he went to preschool and we were all so excited when he recognized his letters, and then when he knew what sound they made. Those preschool years were some of the best in my whole life. Roger was working at the warehouse then, so I had a little space to breathe. I'd drop Lucas off at preschool, then do my errands—go to the grocery store, take the cat to the vet, or go home and do laundry. I was always careful to be mindful of my time.

That was before—well not completely before, maybe that was when things started going bad. When my independence started to be hard on Roger. When I had to learn what it meant to be part of a family, part of a team.

Once, on my birthday, I went to the mall and got my nails done, got a milkshake and window shopped. It was a little piece of heaven. A tiny little slice of what life was like before having a baby. Even all these years later I remember that feeling of freedom. I felt so happy, and so lucky—I couldn't even remember the last time I had done something like that.

But then after I got home, and after dinner, Roger noticed my fingernails. When he asked, I told him about my little treat for myself and how nice it was. Why was my "freedom" so important to me? It always ended up with Roger and me fighting about it. I know marriage is supposed to be work—I know that from all the magazines that write about relationships and how it is not supposed to be easy all the time. You have to put the work in to make a marriage last. But I think maybe I just wasn't cut out for all that work. Because sometimes I didn't want to do all that, I just wanted freedom—I just wanted to be able to feel like I could breathe. I'd forget to let him know where I was and what I was doing and it was hard on him to worry about me like that, especially if I was out with Lucas and he didn't know where we were. It felt suffocating to me sometimes—often really. So I try to remember the good parts— Lucas's chubby little fingers as he held the crayons while he was drawing, Lucas just after his nighttime bath, smelling of shampoo and wearing his pajamas with feet.

Across from me, Bonnie-Lynn is using her finger to point to each letter while she slowly says its name and then its sound. She is concentrating hard, her forehead wrinkled in thought, just like Lucas. It makes me laugh, that similarity.

"What's funny?" Bonnie-Lynn asks, her eyes narrowing.

"Sorry," I say. "It's just that your expression just now, you looked like my son when he was learning to read."

She raises her eyebrows at me. "Hm." She doesn't seem amused.

We put away our books and plan when to meet next. And as I head back to my cell, I realize that I am smiling. I have done something right. I haven't messed things up, at least not yet. And that feels good.

CHAPTER 19

Jean (2001)

D
r. Scott is thin and wiry. Her eyes look smart and alive, and I can see right away that she is good at her job. Because she makes me feel like I can tell her anything. She doesn't ask me, at first, about that night. She wants me to tell her about what I've been feeling lately and why I went to the doctor that time I told Jonny about. So I do. I tell her about my forgetting things and misplacing things and thinking things moved. I tell her about how I can be so awkward and always say the wrong thing, so I don't have many friends. I tell her about how, when I want to see an old friend, something always comes up with Roger and we end up fighting, and so maybe there is part of me deep down that isn't really able to have friends. I tell her about my anger issues and about how, even now, when it's damn sure hard for me to deny that I am the one with the problem, sittin' here in jail like I am, I still feel so sure I am right about things. Some things at least. I swear, even now I think somehow Roger is the one with the problem, not me. One of us must be crazy, that's for damn sure.

When I am done talking, she has a funny look on her face.

"I already told you that everything you say to me is confidential. I won't tell anyone about anything you've said unless you give me permission to." She motions to the recorder on the table. I had forgotten about it by now. "I'd like to share this interview with your lawyer Jean," she says. "Don't worry, it will still be confidential—he won't be able to share it with anyone else either. Would that be alright with you?"

I shrug. "Sure, I guess so." I can't see any harm to it, but I don't know what good it's gonna do either. Cause I am pretty certain there aint nothing I'm saying that's gonna help my case. Unless I am pleading insanity.

That thought stops me in mid-sentence and I give a little gasp. "Is he gonna plead that I'm insane?" I ask. Despite myself, my eyes fill with tears. "I know I got issues, and sometimes I think I must be going crazy. But if he says that in court, everybody's gonna know."

"Your lawyer won't do anything without you agreeing to it—you talk to him and you can both figure out together the best thing to do. My job is to listen to what you have to say and to recommend whether or not you are fit to stand trial. That's a different question from the question of whether you could plead not guilty by reason of insanity."

"Well," I ask, "You think I'm fit for trial?"

She looks at me. This woman is not gonna sugar coat anything for me, I can see that. "Yes," she nods. There is something funny in her expression that I can't quite figure out. "Yes, Jean, I think you are ready for trial."

I ponder this. "You think I should plead not guilty on account of insanity?"

"That's something your lawyer should talk about with you Jean. I'll make a report back to him, and he can talk with you about what your options are."

The library is quiet. Its smell is comforting. Just a little different from every other place here at the Middleton Correctional Facility. I am here a few minutes early, and I sit at our table after piling a few of the usual books in a stack. I notice how calm I am. I notice how I am not looking at the clock every few minutes wondering if I am late, if I should call Roger to let him know where I am. My hands are not shaking like they do so often.

I ask Bonnie-Lynn, after we've worked for a while, what she's in for.

"They got me on murder," she says. I raise my eyebrows.

She shrugs. "Well, the way I see it is, I got bad taste in men. Don't know why, but I always end up with someone that's trouble. Runs in the family, I guess. I knew this guy was trouble, and I didn't care. Really, at that point in my life, all I wanted was to get high. I got high all the time—sometimes coke, but mostly meth. It's cheaper. You wouldn't have even recognized me back then—I was skinny. Skinny like a stick, like somebody could just break me in two if they wanted to. One night he asks me to drive him to this guy's house. So I did. But I ain't gonna sit in the car and just wait for his ass, so I get outta the car and go in with him."

She shrugs and looks at me like she is done and that is the end of the story. But I want to know what happened. Because to say that I understand how people can snap in an instant and do something they will forever regret is pretty much the understatement of the year.

"What happened?"

She looks at me, and it is as if she sees my need to know that I am not the only one. That I am not alone. There are not many moments of real connection in this place—for the most part we all have to keep our guard up, keep our masks on. But hearing her story makes me in some strange way hopeful. Someone else in this world messed up like I did. I am not alone.

"At first it was all good. We cooked that shit up right there—couldn't even wait to get home we wanted it so bad. Then something went wrong. All I remember is my man and the guy we bought from arguing. Then one of 'em whipped out a gun—I don't know which first—but there are shots, and there's blood, and then Karl handed me a knife in the middle of all that crazy, and when someone came at me, I used it. That's all I can really say about it. I used that knife and I guess I sliced that guy pretty good, 'cause it wasn't much later we were speeding down the road and we heard the sirens. We were both so high, I didn't even think about the knife, and I had it right there in the car with me. Karl, he had chucked the gun out the window or something, but neither of us ever thought about that knife. Didn't matter anyways, since we were high as kites and blood spattered all over. Wouldn'ta made one bit of difference either way."

I watch Bonnie-Lynn. It is not hard to imagine her in a rough situation. But I think maybe she is different now than she was then. That's not hard to imagine either.

She takes a breath and purses her lips. "I meant it when I said I got bad taste in men, but that ain't the whole problem." She shakes her head. "Truth is, I was just a big ole mess—didn't think enough of myself to think I could do anything but what I was doing. I didn't think much at all to be honest."

Our stories are so different, but I feel a pull to hers. It has an ache of emptiness that feels familiar.

"I think that shrink I met with the other day is gonna tell my lawyer I'm crazy," I tell her.

She looks at me with her chin down, and she laughs out loud. "Girl, if you're crazy than they better be getting out the straightjacket for me."

"I forget things sometimes."

"Really? I never known you to forget nothing. I never heard you say anything crazy. Believe me, around here we know crazy. You don't seem fucked up to me."

"Thanks," I smirk. "I'm sure that will help my case with the jury."

CHAPTER 20

Cora (1988)

No matter how many times Cora counted the days on the calendar, the result was the same. In a small town like Abilene, it was nearly impossible to keep a secret. So she drove to the Albertson's thirty miles outside of town, where no one would know her, to buy the pink box. She bought two—thinking she wanted to be absolutely sure. Then she drove the thirty miles back home with her palms sweating and a huge lump in her throat.

At home, she made her way past Ma, who sat in the kitchen with a pungent tea, playing solitaire, letting the cards make a crisp "snap" sound whenever she placed them on the table, and past Bo, in the living room playing Atari with a friend. They didn't even notice her. She headed up the wooden stairs and into the ancient bathroom on the second floor. She followed the instructions and spent the most excruciating ten minutes of her life. Waiting. She refused to let herself look at the tube ahead of time so as not to believe something false before the result. She willed herself not to look at the test strip—one line for no, two lines for yes. She wondered, was it blank until the results appeared, or was there one line right away and you just waited to see if that second line would show? She made herself wait a full minute longer than it said on the box, just to be sure—focusing on the paint peeling in the corners of the ceiling and on the ancient radiator that noisily heated the room in the winter.

When she saw the two pink lines, she was not surprised. She had known all along really.

Coralee was not a hick—she knew how these things worked. Shit, she had been on the pill for over a year just so she didn't have to worry about crap like this. She hadn't asked him to use a condom—it would have seemed so base, so practical that it would have ruined the magic. But she remembered Thornton Rushmore—her first lay at a frat party—who had said, with authority, "Real men use condoms" as if he was giving her a gift. He was tender and sweet, and when she went on her way and never saw him again, she didn't have to worry about a thing.

Maybe real men did use condemns. She remembered how polite Thornton had been afterwards—getting her a drink of water, and a warm washcloth. She always figured that was why she had slept with him in the first place—he was just so darn polite about it. She'd never been with a jock before and she was curious. When she'd thought about that line before in her life—"real men use condoms"—she'd only ever laughed at it. She'd laughed with her girlfriends at the inflated head of someone who would say something like that. It wasn't until she sat thinking about those two pink lines, that she realized the truth in what he had said, the maturity and thoughtfulness behind his politeness. She realized that when he married, his wife would be a lucky woman.

But it did her no good to think of these things now—to beat herself up for being so stupid, so naive. She remembered how when she went camping for four days with her friends she'd forgotten to bring her pills with her.

But, she was not a hick, and she knew how to handle something like this. There were four weeks left of summer break. Four weeks left for her to take care of her situation and pull herself together enough to head back to school. So she called the clinic in Sweetwater and made an appointment. They asked if she had someone to drive her home, and Cora said no. She didn't want anyone with her. She would never tell anyone.

Cora sat in the waiting room at the clinic, surrounded by posters of healthy, happy women and children. Except for her and the cheerful receptionist behind the counter, the room was empty. Cora was glad. She wanted to be alone. She did not want to talk to the chirpy receptionist, she did not want to talk to the nurse who invited her back and took her pulse and weighed her and made no-nonsense notes on a sheet inside her manila folder. And she especially did not want to talk to the doctor who she was told (after she dutifully peed in the cup provided) would be right in.

Cora sat, her bare ass covered in all directions with crinkly paper, and for a moment felt extremely sorry for herself. She felt the sadness welling up within her like a wave gathering height. She tried to push the thought of Edison out of her mind. The image of the happy, shiny woman in the poster rose up, unbidden, the baby in her arms, making her complete, radiant. She imagined for a moment, Edison sitting on her doorstep waiting for her when she returned home, explaining how he had been in a car accident and had had temporary amnesia, and as soon as he returned to his senses he had rushed back to her side. She imagined, for one tiny moment, him holding a baby in his arms, his face radiant and shiny like the woman in the poster. Her baby. Their baby. And in spite of Cora attempting to push all these images out of her brain, and in spite of her pressing her thumbnail into her palm so hard she almost drew blood, the tears began to slide down her face.

It was the most inopportune moment possible for the doctor to walk in. Five minutes earlier, and Cora would have been composed and matter-of-fact. Five minutes later and she would have pulled herself together and been again composed and matter of fact. But, the entry of the doctor, with her kind face and clean white coat, instead of bringing Cora back from the brink of misery, somehow propelled her toward it, and when she saw the concern in the doctor's face, the wave that had been rising in Cora's chest suddenly gained momentum and burst forth, leaving her to heave big gasps of breath through her tears.

The doctor closed the door gingerly behind her, as if intentionally making all her movements gentle so as not to upset Cora further.

"I'm sorry," Cora stammered. "I'm fine," she insisted, desperately wiping her eyes.

The doctor looked at her, then glanced down at the clipboard she held in her hands. "It's OK," she said, looking up again and placing the clipboard down on the counter. She sat across from her.

"Well, the first thing I can tell you is, the test was positive, you are pregnant.

Cora nodded. It struck her that all the time she'd been sitting there, she'd never even questioned the pink lines she'd seen on her home test.

She looked down at her chart again. "And it looks like you are only a few weeks along. You still have an array of options in front of you."

"I don't need to hear my options. I'm ready."

The doctor raised her eyebrows slightly.

"It doesn't look like you've been to our counseling session yet, right?"

Cora shook her head.

"We just want to make sure you have all the information regarding your options, before you make the decision about what you want to do. That's why, before we schedule any abortion procedure, we require a counseling session first."

"I don't need counseling. I know what I want to do. I have to go back to school. I can't have a baby right now. It's just not an option."

"OK," the doctor nodded again, unshakably calm. "But we do have these requirements. If we don't do it in every case, we could lose our funding, you see. So this visit, what's going to happen is, we will do an examination, make sure everything is fine, and you and I will talk a little about your options. Even if you know them already, I am required to tell you about them."

Cora nodded. She dutifully let the doctor examine her. And she listened as she talked about adoption possibilities, and financial assistance available for unemployed mothers, and as she described the abortion procedure, complete with pictures so she would understand completely. But Cora knew what she was doing. She nodded and listened and held her resolve.

And then the doctor wanted her to talk. She asked if the father knew. She asked if Cora had family nearby and support. And at the end, Cora made another appointment a few days later when they would perform the procedure. Then she drove home.

As soon as she walked into the house, she smelled the sage. Her mother stood at the stove, stirring something that bubbled loudly.

Ma turned and looked at her. "Sit, Cora," she said softly. I made you some tea."

Suddenly Cora felt she was a little girl again. Looking to her mother to make everything all right, to help her out of a mess she had made. She sat at the table and Ma put a steaming mug in front of her. She sat next to her, reached out and stroked her hair. Somehow, her mother just knew.

"It will be okay darling," Ma said softly.

Cora couldn't look at her. She knew she would have to talk about it now.

"You know, I like that boy," Ma said, sipping her tea. "He loves you. I can tell."

"If he loved me, I don't think he would have left town without even leaving me a number, without even saying goodbye."

"I am never wrong about these things. You know that honey."

Cora did know that, and it was this pronouncement, this certainty that opened up her heart. She had known it too. But then why did he just leave? When she asked her mother this most basic of questions, it was the one thing her mother did not have an answer to.

They kept sitting at the kitchen table.

"I'm pregnant," Cora said.

"I know," said her ma.

"I don't know what to do."

Ma reached over and put a hand on Cora's stomach. It was flat as a pancake, and did not seem any different from a month ago, but it was as if an electric pulse came out of that hand and warmed her. And she felt that all would somehow be okay. People got pregnant all the time—it wasn't like it was the fifties and she had to be shipped off to some Home for Unwed Mothers or something.

"What should I do?" she asked.

But Cora's mother just stroked her hair as if she were a little girl. "You'll figure it out," she said. "You decide what you want to do, and I will be right here beside you, whatever it is."

The next morning, Cora woke early, just as the sun was beginning to climb in the sky. She didn't have to be at work until 10:00 to open up (things were pretty laid back at the video store) so she walked barefoot out of the house and down to the creek.

By the time she got to the creek there was enough of a hint of the heat ahead that the cool water felt good on her feet. The stones were smooth, and she walked gingerly out to the middle, where the water still only came halfway up her calves. It felt so good, that after a few minutes she bent down, splashing her legs. She ended up sitting in the water in her pajama shorts— just sitting there letting the cool water flow over her as if she were just another rock in the way, listening to its soft gurgle and the birds chirping as the rest of the ranch woke up.

It was a Tuesday, but she knew she would not go to the Upstairs Lounge that night. She was fairly certain she would never go there again. Even when she went back to Georgetown, which she fully intended to do whatever decision she made, she knew that she would not go clubbing like she used to. Sometimes she wondered if she had chosen Georgetown only because of the DC scene. There, she could go shopping at Commander Salamander and Classic Clothing. She could hang out at the 9:30 Club and the other dives that people at her school would never understand—Poseurs, Carmichael's, Tracks. She had a friend who was local, who knew all the bouncers and since she happened to be drop-dead gorgeous in a Siouxsie sort of way, they always let her in for free, no matter the line. She and Cora would hop from club to club, flashing a smile to get in (or not if it was cool instead of flirty that would get them in).

Cora lived the life—she studied hard, which her club friends didn't understand, and she partied hard, which her school friends didn't understand. The students partied in their own, soft way. Kegs of beer and the occasional foray out into the club scene, but they always ended up drinking with the frat boys at Crazy Horse (a joke to her club friends). They drank until they threw up, and bemoaned their hangovers and talked about how hard they partied on Friday night. But they did not know what it was like to drop acid and go skinny dipping at the pool in Dumbarton Oaks at four in the morning, or be Xing so hard you danced for six hours straight and still couldn't sleep, even at 10:00 the next morning. Cora knew it wasn't a lifestyle she could sustain. She didn't imagine she would live that life forever. But she felt that each experience expanded her mind. She wasn't sure she could understand Heidegger or Husserl half so well if she had not had those doors of perception thrown wide open with chemical help.

But now she felt a fundamental shift in her being—as if she had aged ten years in the past week. It was not a momentary feeling. The shift was at her core. She was simply a different person now.

Cora sat and thought about her life. There was so much she wanted to do. She wanted to get her degree and go to graduate school. She wanted to travel the world. Other than that though, she could not be specific. She had no desire to get some job just for the sake of getting a job. She was pretty certain she'd end up in academia—get her Ph.D. and end up a professor somewhere. She always thought that idea had been planted by her father. It was what he thought he should have done, in the end when he was looking back on his life. She regretted now that she had never asked him why he hadn't. She wondered, with a pang, whether it had been because of her and Bo. She didn't think so though. Really, why should having a baby keep you from doing whatever you want to do. Obviously, there was the time issue—she knew babies needed around the clock care. But they do grow up right? They go to school during the day when they are older. There are plenty of parents that work full time jobs and have kids.

For a moment—just a tiny, fleeting moment, she thought about scoring some X and going to the Upstairs Lounge tonight anyway. But before the thought even completely came to her, she had rejected it. She did not need chemical help. She did not need the throb of the bass and the excitement of a wide-open world to get her blood pumping and feel alive. She needed only the warm field outside, with the soft scent of sage in the wind and the distant nostril noise of the horses. She needed only her mother's arms open wide, her brother, her family around her. And she knew, without a doubt now, that she needed the little life inside of her to grow. That it would become the center of her universe, where nothing else would matter to her ever again—not school, not boys, not drinks, not even Heidegger or Nietzsche. Well, maybe Heidegger just a little bit.

She let herself imagine, for a moment, what the baby inside her might look like. She wondered if it would have Edison's eyes. Cora wasn't conscious of time. She had no idea how long she sat there in the water. But when she stood up and waded back to the creek bed, her toes were wrinkled. The sun was warm on her back as she walked slowly to the house.

CHAPTER 21

Cora (1988)

Strange that one of the hardest things of all was telling Tessa. Cora put it off and put it off, as the long summer days began to shorten, and as her mornings became a blur of nausea, saltine crackers, Jell-O, and peppermint tea. She put it off as the bills for the semester came, and she called to let the registrar know she would not be returning. And still, she could not call Tessa.

"Oh my God—get out!" Tessa screamed as soon as Cora told her. "I'm freaking out!"

"I know."

"I can't believe it, I mean. Really, Cora, I'm totally freaking out right now! Why didn't you call me? I would have come down to get you—take you to Planned Parenthood or something. We can still do it. It's not too late."

"I don't want to, Tessa. I'm keeping it. I'm having the baby." And it sounded real to Cora, not unusual or traumatic. It was just her life.

There was silence on the other end, as Tessa was stunned. "Wow." And then, "Oh my God, I am going to get this kid the cutest clothes!"

Cora laughed, imagining the tiny leather jacket and Doc Martens Tessa would send.

Then her friend was serious. "But Cora, you can't just give up your degree. Just defer for a year or something. Come back with the baby—we'll all babysit and stuff. Jeez, you can't just quit—what are you going to do, live on that farm for the rest of your life?"

"I don't know." And she meant that. She couldn't truly imagine living out the rest of her days on a cattle farm—wearing her "Meat is Murder" T-shirt was not just theoretical where she was raised.

But still, three months after he had left, every time the phone rang, her heart did a little flip. Sometimes, she'd get hang-up calls. Always, she wondered if it was him. She wondered if she just blurted out "I'm pregnant" as soon as she picked up the phone, instead of saying hello, whether there would be any reaction. But she never did it.

Cora vowed she would not go soft. She would not be the fat woman pacing the aisles of the Piggly Wiggly, her hands sticky and shirt stained, begging her red-faced child to hold on just a little while longer so she could stock up on Little Debbie Snack Cakes without a tantrum, promising she would give her a lollipop, take her to McDonalds, anything just to stave off a screaming fit. She vowed not to be that woman.

She kept working at the video store, knowing she was abundantly overqualified, but not wanting to apply for other jobs with her stomach crouched at the starting line and just waiting to sprint into high maternity gear within weeks.

In the evenings she'd sit in the kitchen, working slowly on the batch of beans her mother placed in front of her to shell, or watching her fry chicken. She tried to chase off the feeling that her life had stalled. She felt it sputtering every day, but kept on, reading the texts she'd purchased for the classes she would have taken if she'd gone back. Bo was taking classes at Texas State Tech and working in the shop. The irony was that he would end up with a degree before she did. A degree from Tech, but still, it suited him well. He was always tinkering, ever since he was little. And he wanted to be out and working with his hands, not sitting at a desk all day. That's what he always said.

Bo was moving forward. Everyone she knew was moving forward. And so was she—she knew that. It was just that she was facing a different direction now.

CHAPTER 22

Len (2001)

R achel and I find the new album by Clifton Wilkes at Sam Goody—it is not out in front displayed with the new releases, but it is right there where it's supposed to be, in the bins in alphabetical order. On the bus trip home, I hold that plastic bag tightly. I can feel the album, heavy with promise, and I force myself to leave it in the bag. It is all I can do to stop myself from ripping it open right there. But I want to wait. I want to wait until I am home and in my room, to pull it out and examine once again the picture on the cover—the chiseled profile, frustratingly obscure. I want to take my time before listening to the record.

Dusty air blows through the half-opened window, and the seat is sticky against my bare legs. Rachel sits beside me, growing more serious as we near home.

"Let's go to your house to listen instead of mine," she says.

"Sure," I say.

"Ma's getting worse," she says as the bus stop comes into view up ahead. "I don't know if I can stand it much longer. I'm probably gonna go live with my dad soon."

I nod. I've been hearing that same line ever since Rachel and her mom moved next door to us two years ago. "I'll tell Ma to go over and check on her," I say.

Rachel shrugs. I know it won't do much either, but it's all I got.

The bus squeaks to a stop just outside of Buck's.

"Let's get a Pepsi," Rachel says.

Buck's Country Store has everything you ever might need in Abilene. Rolls of barbed wire, all kinds of lumber out back, cans of soup and vegetables, and a whole separate room for guns and all the stuff that goes with them. But the best thing about Buck's is the candy beside the front counter. There is a low table set out, and on top of it are bins filled with Mary Janes, Bazooka bubble gum, tootsie rolls, and caramels with that white stuff in the middle.

We walk through the dusty white door with peeling paint. Rachel heads straight over to the soda machine in the back. But I take a minute to wander down the aisles, looking at the salt licks, barrels of feed, and ancient canned goods—the smell is sweet and dusty. I turn down an aisle crammed with halters, lead ropes, and saddle soap, and I feel somehow as though everything looks just a little bit different. Like now that I know who my daddy is, I have a slightly different perspective. I am not a little kid anymore, racing to the candy bins.

When I get to the end of the aisle, I see Rachel at the counter, leaning her elbows on it and talking to Buck Junior. Buck Senior is clearly not the most creative person when it comes to names, because there is also a dog that sits out front named Dog. Rachel tips her head back and laughs at something Buck says, and I think again how she sure does look like a movie star—somehow she knows how to lean just the right way in her cutoff jeans and tip her head back just the right amount when she laughs. Buck's a goner, that much is clear.

I grab a handful of Mary Janes, bring them over and plop them on the counter. Buck raises his eyebrows at me like he had no idea I was even here.

"I was just setting Buck straight here," Rachel says. "That Roger might end up being just fine—they still don't know for sure, so we shouldn't be talkin' about Jean going away for life or something like that."

I raise my eyebrows and Buck looks sheepish. I shrug. "Yeah, they just don't know yet."

We walk out with our Pepsi's and Mary Janes, and head toward home.

Rachel says, "How are they even your aunt and uncle anyway? Your Ma's only brother is Bo."

"Yeah, but Bo's married to Cisley, so she's my aunt. And then her sister is Jean, and Jean is married to Roger. So I guess that makes them my aunt and uncle, too—or at least that's what I always called them."

Rachel looks skeptical. "I don't know—that doesn't even sound like real family to me."

"Well here in Abilene, that's family."

The sun is warm and the Pepsi is cold, and I have a good feeling as we walk along the dusty road back home. It is as if the universe is suddenly aligned properly. I feel the song inside of me start to hum a little bit, and I wish I could say the words of the perimeter for Rachel's mom. But I have tried that before already. It doesn't seem to work that way—I can't see Mrs. Corbin's black clouds the way I can see Ma's, and my saying the words or sending out my song doesn't seem to have any effect.

But I feel so good as I walk beside Rachel, and I think maybe this time somehow it will be different. Maybe if I send out my song to Mrs. Corbin, by the time Rachel gets home later she'll be freshly showered and dressed up nice and cooking an omelet. But there is another feeling too, as I feel the weight of the album in the Sam Goody bag. And suddenly it's not even a conscious choice, I just can't help myself. That song inside starts to bubble up—stronger the more I think of my father. As I walk there is a rhythm, and with the rhythm my insides start to hum, and I feel it, like waves, and I am light and airy and beautiful. I lose track of the steps I am taking, forget completely even what road I am on and where I am going.

It is only when I feel Rachel's hand on my arm, pressing me as if I should stop walking that I come back to myself. I hadn't even realized that my eyes were closed.

"Shhh—don't move," whispers Rachel.

I stand still, my eyes still closed, and feel the breath of the universe all around me. It is whisper soft against my skin, like a tiny, fluttering heartbeat all around me. Slowly I open my eyes, and there is orange. Orange all around. The butterflies don't land, they dip and flutter, and then continue on their way up along the road and into the distance, in a cluster that morphs and changes like a beautiful drunken starlet.

We keep walking. Thoughtful.

"Len, we should just go find Clifton Wilkes. We can run away—take the bus, or hitchhike or something," Rachel says as we near her house. "Your ma's not gonna change her mind."

I shrug. "She might."

Rachel raises her eyebrows at me, skeptical.

"And anyway," I say, "the way I figure, once I write that letter to my dad, he'll have to come, won't he?"

W e try to sneak in the house quietly—I don't want to share the album with anyone except Rachel.

"Are you girls back already? How was the pool?" Ma calls out as we pass her study. I peak my head in. She is working on her 'thesis' again—I can tell by the four thick volumes open on the tables surrounding her and the pages of handwritten notes spread out on her desk.

"We ended up going to the mall instead," I say, holding the Sam Goodie bag outside of the doorway so she can't see it.

"Okay, well do me a favor—include Lucas a bit will you? I feel so terrible for him and nothing I try to do seems to help."

"Okay," I say. "But later—first we have some things we have to try on."

She nods and turns back to her desk, her red pen clutched tightly.

Rachel and I practically run into my room, and I peel the plastic wrap off the album.

Rachel plops onto my bed. "I wish it was the kind that has a flap you can open and a bunch of pictures inside."

"Me too," I say. I also wish they would take an honest to goodness photo and not try to be all artsy about it because the cowboy hat covers most of Clifton's face, and it's just his profile anyway. But all the same, I dig the polaroid out of my drawer. I sit down beside Rachel on the bed and we examine both photos carefully until we are sure.

"It's definitely him," Rachel says.

I nod. But really, if I hadn't seen him on TV I would never have known. You really can't tell anything by the album photo.

I gingerly slide the record out from the sleeve and carry it over to my record player. It is warm in my hands, and I can feel it, already calling out to me—I can feel it pulsing through my fingertips.

My hands shake just a little as I place it on the turntable. The needle sputters.

At the sound of the guitar, my heart feels more steady in my chest. When the piano joins it, I can feel my breath—feel the air as it comes into my lungs and fills them. My whole body is waiting for the next moment. And when it happens, when I hear his voice, it is familiar, as if it were a part of me that I am finally reunited with, and at the same time it is foreign and beautiful, a sound I have been waiting for my whole life. I don't really even hear the words, just the sound, just the melody, and it begins to merge with the song inside of me, that has been there waiting for such a long time.

When the song ends, Rachel raises her eyebrows. "It's good," she says.

The next song comes on.

"This is so cool Len," she says.

I nod, but my throat is tight, and I can't actually bring myself to say anything in response.

By the third song, Lucas appears in the doorway. "What are you listening to?" he asks. I show him the album cover—I don't mention anything about who Clifton is—and he nods, sits on my floor and listens with us.

Granny appears next in the doorway, and then Bo, who I didn't even know was over, and finally, by the time the last song finishes, Ma stands in the doorway, her arms crossed and her brow furrowed, staring at the record player.

The needle runs its course and there is an empty, scratchy sound until I reach over and replace it.

Ma still stares at the record player. "Guys, I'd like to talk to Len for a moment if you don't mind."

They slowly scatter—Rachel says "see you later" before she heads home, and the rest of them melt back into other parts of the house.

Ma comes over and sits beside me on my bed. She reaches out for the album cover, and I hand it to her. She stares at it a long time, her lips pressed together.

"Okay Len, I have to tell you something."

I just sit, feeling the breath coming in and out. I still feel the music deep inside of me. It is like that album is replaying again, right in the place where I breathe.

"You're right. This is your father." She runs a hand over the photo on the cover of the album—the chiseled profile topped with a cowboy hat.

"Yeah, I kind of figured that already."

"I sure wasn't looking for a Clifton Wilkes all this time."

"Yeah, I figured that part too."

"Well, I have to think about what to do here Len. There are things that make the situation complicated. It's not like I can just call him up or something. I'll have to give all this some thought."

"Well I don't. I've been giving this situation some thought for my whole entire life. I don't have to think about it anymore, we just need to go and find him. He doesn't even know I exist—we have to tell him."

"I'm afraid it just might not be that easy honey."

I feel a pang in my chest, a tightening. Because I have not forgotten that she said I was a mistake. And I wonder, as she pats my shoulder and leaves the room, if that might be partly why she doesn't want to contact him—I wonder if she just doesn't want him to know about this mistake.

CHAPTER 23

Len (2001)

That album is the last thing I listen to when I go to bed that night, and it is the first thing I listen to when I wake up the next morning before dawn. I turn the volume down low and get right next to the speaker so no one else can hear it.

There has been a shift in the air in our house. I can feel it so clearly. There was always a question floating in the air, my whole life. And now it is not so much a question, it is more like waiting for a solution. Before I put my barn boots on, I want to feel what the earth has to say to me. I slip outside, my feet bare, and dig my toes into the dirt beside the steppingstones. I stand on the lush grass beside the pathway, and I can feel a thrum in the air around me. I can feel the earth and the stones, singing out to me, and it feels the same as always—it is not different. But I am different. I am stronger, I am more sure.

I ride the perimeter and it is uneventful. My song hums inside of me, but it is soft, it does not need to come out today.

I'm sitting at the table with Ma eating toast when Lucas comes into the kitchen. He wears faded jeans and a T-shirt and his hair is a little tousled.

"Good morning Lucas," Ma says brightly, standing up. "Now while you're here, I don't want you to feel like a guest. You're family, so you just jump right in here and help yourself to anything you like in the kitchen at any time, ok?"

He nods and looks around.

"I can make you some eggs," she says. "Or we have toast, or cereal."

He just walks over to the coffee pot, pulls a mug off the counter above, and pours himself a cup of coffee. "Thanks, but I'm good with this," he says.

When he heads back out of the kitchen with his cup, Ma widens her eyes at me.

I shrug. It's like the reason he's here is this big unspoken cloud hanging over him. I'm not quite sure whether we should all just pretend it isn't there and act like things are normal, or try to bust through and talk about it.

"Just take him down to the creek or something this morning, will you?" she whispers to me. "I feel so bad for him, and I just don't know what to do."

And so I do—later that morning I watch Lucas lose some racing game on the play station over and over again. After about his fifteen millionth crash I say, "Ma says I'm supposed to take you down to the creek."

"Hmm," he grunts as he starts a new game.

"I don't know, I think she just wants to make sure you get out of house at some point."

After the next crash he shrugs and says "Okay" and puts away his controller.

The creek is about a fifteen-minute walk out into the north pasture. I lead the way along the narrow path. Before we get to the split rail fence, the landscape is lush and green. The path is lined with steppingstones, but still we have to push aside the blue vervain and scarlet monkey flowers that grow beside it. But once we pass through the gate, the landscape changes and we walk on dirt, trying not to kick up too much dust as we go. There is sage on the hillside and some red yucca plants here and there, but most of the rest of the ranch is flat and brown, hosting mostly crabgrass and tumbleweed.

Lucas and I walk along, the late morning sun already fierce and beating down on us. Down by the creek there is a little breeze, and the water is nice and cool, especially in the shade. We take off our shoes and socks, roll up our pants, and stick our feet in the water. I scrunch up my toes, letting the mud ooze all in between them and up around my feet. When we were little Lucas and I would come down here to go wading and we'd splash and run around, but we are older now, and we are weighted down, both of us, so I just sink my toes in the mud for a while.

I wait for a bit and take a deep breath. "Have you seen your mama yet?" I ask.

"Just once," he replies, moving out of the creek and sitting on the grass. "She said on the phone that she don't want me to see her in prison." He digs into his pocket and pulls out a pack of Marlboros and a lighter. He tilts the package toward me, offering me one, but I shake my head, trying to look cool about it.

I sit beside him, my hands crossed over my knees, and I smell the sharp smoke as he lights the cigarette. We watch the clouds for a few minutes.

"What about your dad?" I ask.

He nods. "I seen him once. I mean, my dad don't know that. He's unconscious, hooked up to all these tubes and stuff." He shrugs. "I don't know. I heard the doctor said he might not make it."

"I'm sorry," I tell him. I don't know what else to say.

He shrugs again, sits up and twists his cigarette out into the dirt. "Let's head back. I'm hungry."

We walk back along the same path, kicking up dust. The green circle, the jungle around our house, gets closer. It isn't only green, there are white and blue flowers, and vines bursting with hot pink over the fences. And as always, the banana tree, rising above it all.

"I got a match coming up next month," he says as we walk. "It's a summer wrestling league—the school team doesn't start til September."

"Oh yeah?"

"My ma always takes me to those. Most other kids, their dads are there, yelling at 'em, cheering and stuff."

"Maybe your dad's just been busy," I say.

He nods. "That's what he usually says."

I know I should be focused on Lucas. I know his situation is way worse than mine no matter how you look at it. But I can't help it—I feel a little stab of jealousy that he's all along had a father. Even if he's too busy to take him to tournaments, at least he's been around. And least they know each other.

Later, Lucas is glued to his video games, Ma is out running errands, and I use the computer in the study to find out all I can about Clifton Wilkes. There does not really seem to be much out there about him, the news is surprisingly sparse. But I find all the details about his recent album release, and, most importantly, I come across the list of his upcoming tour dates.

It is not really my fault that I see Ma's email. I am not trying to snoop. I click on a screen that is minimized, and suddenly, there is Ma's draft e-mail up on the screen. It is addressed to "sarah@cliftonwilkesfanclub.com." Really if you want something to be a secret, you need to be a little more careful. And anyway, if we are reduced to writing to the fan club instead of to the man himself then this is surely an endeavor that could use some assistance. So I read it. I read Ma telling this person about how she has never been able to get hold of Clifton—how she has been looking for him all this time under his real name, Edison. I read about how she didn't know his real last name so that made him pretty difficult to find. She goes on to tell her about how Clifton has this daughter, and she needs to let him know.

I read that thing through. There are some parts that need a little help—like the part about not knowing his last name. Because that right there just sounds ridiculous. I already know it is ridiculous—I've spent lots of time wondering how a person can have a baby with someone and not even know their last name. So I certainly wouldn't expect someone else to understand it—that bit of information might just derail the whole effort. So I change that part for her and I add a couple of other things about how great that daughter is—how she can ride like the wind and how she can shoot an arrow straight to the center of the target every single time. Then, I don't give myself time to second guess, or to read it over one more time. Ma never signed her name at the bottom, so I do it for her and I add our phone number. Then, I press "send."

It is late afternoon by the time Rachel comes over. I have been keeping my eye on Ma since she got home. She hasn't even been in the study yet, but I know it is only a matter of time before she sees what I sent. My only hope is that she gets a response back, and that it's a good one, because I know she will not be happy about what I've done. So when Rachel comes over I don't even mention it. I will just cross that bridge with Ma when I come to it.

The first thing Rachel and I have to do is listen to that album all over again.

We are about halfway through when Lucas knocks on the door to my room. He sits on the floor, and I can tell he is trying to look cool. I can tell he is trying not to stare at Rachel.

"Does he know?" Rachel asks me, her eyes alight with the secret.

I shake my head. And I know she is dying to, so I say, "You can tell him."

Rachel doesn't ride. She's never milked a cow. And she doesn't know how to tell which mushrooms are the ones that will kill you. But Rachel knows how to tell a story better than anyone I've ever met. So she tells the story—even the parts she's only heard from me, and even though it is my story she's telling, I am on the edge of my seat along with Lucas.

"You sure it's him?" he asks me, his head cocked.

I nod. "Ma even admitted it finally."

"Wow." He turns the album over in his hands, the edges of his mouth pulling down. "Dang."

I nod. Rachel's got him beat in the speech department, that's for sure.

"Yeah, and I say if your Ma's not gonna do anything, we should just go find him and tell him ourselves," Rachel says.

"I can't run away," I say.

Rachel shrugs. "But it's not really running away. Going to find you father is not the same thing as running away."

"Sounds like it might be your only shot," Lucas says.

"Maybe," I say. But I picture my Ma and Granny sick with worry. I think about the time I was four years old and fell off the rowboat out on Lake Kirby. How Walter was with us that day and how I barely even hit the water before his large hands reached out to grab me and pull me back on board. How he would not let go of the back of my shirt the entire rest of the time we were on that boat. And that gives me pause, because I just don't know if I have it in me to hurt them like that.

CHAPTER 24

Jean (2001)

Here's the thing we're grappling with Jean," Jonny says, his face serious. He folds his fingers together and leans on the table a little so his arms make a triangle shape. "We can't find any evidence of this woman you say Roger was with. The detectives have been working on it. But they haven't come up with anything yet. Roger's doing better. He's still in a coma, but they're expecting him to improve any day now." He looks down, studying his fingers before he looks at me again. "The thing is, his family is adamant that he was not with another woman."

I stare at him for a minute in disbelief. "That doesn't make any sense."

He shrugs. "That's what they're claiming."

"What about like fingerprints, or DNA or something?" I ask. "I mean, they were having sex, isn't there some DNA on him or something?"

"Well, to be honest, folks were worried about saving his life, not collecting DNA. It was a crime scene and all, but since you were the one that called, and you were also the one standing there with the gun in your hand when they got there, really the focus was on trying to save Roger, not collect DNA samples from his body. It just wasn't something anyone thought they'd need."

"Well, somebody must have seen her. I mean, she ran outta the house half-dressed and all." I try to remember the details. I can picture her face, white with shock and fear, "She was screaming," I say. "But maybe that was me screaming." That part I can't honestly remember.

He shakes his head. "There's a neighbor that says after she heard the shot, she looked out the window and she saw a car driving down the street, but she didn't see it coming out of your driveway, just on the road, and she doesn't remember anything about it, not even the color."

Jonny's face gets serious. "What it means, Jean, is that they are charging you with premeditated attempted murder, not a crime of passion which is second degree. We thought all along it was going to be, worst case, second degree." He folds his fingers together and lets out a breath. "It makes the defense that much harder if the prosecution is contesting your story that there was a woman there."

I stare at him. I hear what he is saying, and I know it is important. But it is hard for me to concentrate. I may be a mess sometimes, but I know what I saw. I think about Roger getting better instead of dying. I am not ready to think about that yet—it makes me feel numb.

Rather than think about that, rather than think about the twenty years in prison I'm told I might be facing, I think about the other times I suspected Roger was with another woman. I remember the first time—not the first time I suspected, but the first time that I was certain, even though he wouldn't admit it.

I remember lying in bed and watching the clock as it turned to 12:00 midnight. He had called around dinner time to tell me he had to work late and I shouldn't wait up. So I knew I shouldn't worry. But I wondered—what time should I start worrying? I went ahead and got ready for bed and I crawled under the covers. I didn't sleep much, waiting for him to come home. The clock turned to 1:00 and then 2:00.

I thought about how he'd been acting toward me lately. He'd told me a few times he was worried about my health because of my weight gain. Was it really that much? Because I still felt pretty good, and when I looked in the mirror, I thought I looked just fine for a mom my age. I'd filled out a bit, that was true. OK, if I was going to be completely honest, I weighed about twenty pounds more than I did when we got married. But I was young and pretty darn skinny to begin with, and twenty pounds is not that big a deal is it? But he'd stopped hugging me, stopped kissing me except when he wanted to have sex. And even then, it never really felt like he wanted me in particular, just that he wanted sex—it could have been with anybody.

Maybe it's partly because I started to smell. I reckoned my sense of smell was messed up or something, 'cause I didn't even smell it—to me I seemed just fine. But he told me, quietly, like he felt bad telling me about it, after I asked him once how come he never hugged or kissed me anymore. He would let me hug him, let me kiss him, but he basically just held himself still when I did, like he was doing me a favor. He got a little sheepish when I asked him, like he was embarrassed, and then he said, "I hate to say anything Jean—but it is real hard for me to stand the way you smell sometimes."

So I started showering three times a day. Even between those showers I would put on extra deodorant and lotions that smelled like fruit or coconut. I didn't put on perfumes cause I tried that before and he couldn't stand it—it made him cough something fierce, and he said that was worse than the other. And I never walked over to him to hug him or kiss him. I would find myself staying just a little away from him, terrified that I stunk.

I watched the clock move to 3:00 and then 4:00. So I thought to myself, maybe he met some girl at work. Someone with a hard, fit body, who smells good and smiles and says the right thing all the time. By 5:00 I was convinced he was having an affair, and I thought, maybe I should just go on and get a divorce. Maybe I'd be better off on my own, like I used to be. Then I remembered that I used to be able to handle things, but I wasn't like that anymore. I'd have to get a job and then what would I do with Lucas while I was at work? And Roger had said before how he would never get a divorce. Never in a million years. It would mean he was a loser, a failure, and he would never be that no matter what he had to do.

But there was that anger inside me that popped up. And I felt like, if I did up and leave, how free I would feel. For a moment I let myself imagine that freedom. I could go to my ma's. I'd be embarrassed, and I'd feel like a failure, but she would take me in, there was no question in my mind. But even as I let myself think it, I knew without a doubt, that that would never happen. I knew, without even completely finishing the thought in my head, that if I tried to take Lucas with me, Roger would fight me tooth and nail. I thought of the case he would make about me being an unfit mother, and I knew I would never try to leave. I vowed instead to try harder. I'd been trying already to make him happy. But apparently, I was not very good at it. So I told myself I would try harder.

A little after 5:30, Roger came quietly into the bedroom. I sat up, my eyes puffy and my head hurting with lack of sleep.

"Sorry honey," he said before I could say anything. He sat down on the edge of the bed, his head hung down. "The car died on my way home."

"What?"

"I don't know what happened to it—it just died and there I was in the middle of nowhere. I couldn't even walk to a gas station to call for help or anything. I waited a while, hoping maybe somebody'd come by to help out or something. I ended up just sleeping in the car. Finally some commuter stopped and gave me a jump—that was all it needed. It brought me home just fine."

I looked at him sort of funny. It just didn't add up. It just didn't fit. But here's the weird thing—part of me was just relieved he was home and lying to me. I knew he was lying, but somehow it felt so much easier than him telling me what I suspected was the truth. I'd been pretending for a pretty long time already. I reckoned I could just go on pretending. But there was also a big part of me that didn't want him to get away with it, that didn't want to be a pansy. I was so tired of being the one who was in the wrong—he should be the one to get called out for messing up once in a while. "Roger," I said, "Are you having an affair?"

He sat up straight and widened his eyes at me like I was crazy. "Oh man," he said shaking his head. His voice had an edge to it when he spoke again. "Jesus—after the night I had, I can't believe you are going to lay into me like this!"

I made sure to keep my voice steady. I made sure I did not yell so he couldn't accuse me of just going off on him. "It just doesn't make any sense Roger," I said. "I mean, why wouldn't you just flag down a car? If you don't want to hitch a ride with them, just ask them to call a tow truck for you at the next gas station or something."

He stood up. His face was set and angry. "I already told you—no one even drove by until about five this morning. You think I wanted to sit there in the car all night? You think this was a fun night for me?" he said. "I don't deserve this shit Jean! I don't deserve these accusations!" He stomped into the bathroom, and I heard him taking a shower.

I let it go. And after an entire day of him giving me the silent treatment, I apologized. I think about that now. Because I am certain, just like I was then, that he was with some other woman that night. And yet I was the one who ended up apologizing to him.

CHAPTER 25

Jean (2001)

I have not seen my friend Mabel in about six years. But there was a time when she was my best friend. Ma had mentioned she wanted to come to visitor's day, so I am not surprised to see her.

She looks good. Maybe lost some weight since I saw her last. There are lines on her face and she looks a little older. But I reckon I must too. That is what happens at our age. A few years can make a world of difference.

Mabel makes her way over to me with her slow, deliberate walk. I remember all those lunch hours we would spend, talking about nothing, laughing so hard over absolutely nothing.

All of a sudden, I get a wave of sadness. It comes over me, hot and unexpected and I have to look away from her. I miss our friendship. I used to just call her up whenever I felt like it. I used to do stuff like meet her for a cup of coffee or to see a movie. That was before I got married. Before I found it just so hard to get away. It was easy to blame it on Lucas—"I'm sorry, I wish I could go to the movies, but I don't think I can leave Lucas tonight." Or, I had to take him to Little League, or help him with his homework. But the truth is, it was just so much easier not to go.

Mabel gives me a small, shy smile and pulls back the metal chair facing my cubicle so she can sit down, her hands folded neatly in her lap. I think about her dainty manners when she eats—holding her fried chicken with the very tips of her fingers. I had forgotten how much I miss her, what a good friend she was.

My eyes water just a little bit and I can't quite say anything yet. I hadn't expected to feel so deeply—she was the one who ended our friendship, and I thought I had gotten over all that. I see the sadness on her face as well, and we are silent for a moment.

She leans forward, leaning her front arms on the table between us. "How are you, Jean?" she asks, then looks down. "I mean…" she looks up at me again. "I just wanted to see you and give you some support."

I remember, as she speaks the words, her concerned expression years ago when Lucas was little and when we were still friends. Her brow would furrow and she'd say "Jean, you tell me—is everything OK? Are you and Roger OK?"

I'd always say I was fine, everything was fine. But something catches in my throat now as I remember it, because I'd always tamped it down before—I'd always pretended otherwise, but inside of me, way deep inside, I knew that it wasn't fine.

"It's good to see you," I say. "I wish it were under different circumstances." That is something you are supposed to say I know—like if you are at a funeral or something. And I want to say the right thing, I want to be careful. Because I miss my friend, and Lord knows I could sure use a friend right about now.

Mabel does something I don't expect. She laughs. A big guffaw right there in the middle of our awkward reunion. "Well that's for damn sure," she says, still laughing, shaking her head. I can't help it—I smile.

"Listen," she says, talking like we just saw each other the other day. "I have wanted to reach out to you so many times over the years. I just…." She purses her lips like she is thinking about what to say. "Maybe it was just my pride. I was hurt when our friendship ended. So whenever I thought maybe I should just call you up, I reminded myself you'd outgrown me. I just let you go. And I will always be sorry for that."

I am not following her. I am sure my confusion shows on my face.

She fidgets, her fingers crossing and uncrossing on the table in front of us. "I mean, I know you felt it was time to move on from our friendship and all, I just keep telling myself now, maybe if I had just called you one more time…"

"What are you talking about?" I shake my head. "I don't even know what you're talking about."

She shrugs, "It's okay. I understand in a way. It was Roger who told me. He said he felt I ought to know." When my face is blank, not understanding, she goes on. "He said you felt you'd outgrown me. He thought he was doing me a favor, you know. I wasn't sure I believed him at first—it just never did sit right with me—but then you never returned my call after I left that message, so I just went on and let you be." She shakes her head. "I just went on with my life and told myself friends grow apart sometimes. But I regret that now. I let you isolate yourself, when I should have been there for you."

There is a thought, the seed of some uneasiness, that starts to grow inside me. I am not sure what it is, but I feel unbalanced, like I might just tip out of my chair at any moment.

I open my mouth as if I'm about to speak. But the words don't come, because I am preoccupied with trying to wrap my brain around what I have just heard.

Mabel nods, pushes back her chair, and stands, heavy on her feet. "It's alright Jean. You don't have to say anything. I'll come back and see you again. We'll talk another day." She turns to go.

"I never said that." I say it quietly, almost to myself.

Mabel turns back.

"I never said anything like that," I go on. "I thought it was you that didn't want to be friends."

Her whole face softens, her whole body, and she sits back down in front of me.

"Why on earth would you think that?"

"Roger told me. He came home one day and told me he had seen you at the store—that before you saw him, he overheard you talking to some other friend about me." I think about how sheepish Roger looked when he was telling me about it, like he didn't want to hurt me but thought I should know. "By then it wasn't just you. I had messed up so many things by that point, I remember thinking I shouldn't be surprised, really."

We just look at each other for a long time, the seed inside me growing slowly. "I never heard any message on my answering machine either," I say.

She shakes her head. "Well Goddamn." I can see the wheels turning as she thinks about it, and I am trying to grasp what this means as well.

"All this time," I say, "All this time Roger lied to us both."

"Look Jean," she leans forward on the table. "I guess in a way all that doesn't matter. I mean…" She looks up and gestures around the room. "Compared to this, that is pretty small potatoes."

We smile for a moment. But then I am serious. "You heard anything about him?" I ask. "I don't get any information in here unless its from my lawyer. I don't even know whether he…." I can't quite bring myself to say it.

She shakes her head. "I don't know."

"They say they're waiting to see how he does before they charge me," I say. But suddenly I don't want to talk about all that. I just want to pretend I am sitting at the diner having coffee with my old friend.

"Tell me about you," I say. "Tell me what's going on in your life." I have so much to say to her, so much to catch up on. But most of it will have to wait for another day, since our time is just about over.

When I am back in my cell, I think about how our friendship ended. Roger never did like Mabel, I always knew that, but he made it sound like he thought she was trying to sabotage our relationship.

I think about other friendships Roger never approved of.

He never said I couldn't see my friends. Never demanded I stay home with him every night. But somehow it was always easier not to go out. There were the few times I had gone to PTA meetings. Whenever I came home Roger would say something like, "Geez—you should have told me you'd be so late, I was starting to really worry." Even if I was an hour earlier than I had said I would be, he would insist I told him 7:00, and I was sure I had said 8:00. But he was always so adamant, so certain. There always seemed to be something he was fuming about. Angry. Really angry because there were clothes left in the dryer so he couldn't do laundry. Really angry because the pots and pans in the kitchen drawer were such a mess that there was no way he could make dinner so he had to order pizza. The counter in the hallway had papers on it that I was going to organize, and he couldn't stand the mess. There was always something. Some reminder of what a disorganized failure I was. Always something I had to apologize for.

In theory, he encouraged me to go out. Especially if someone else was around. I'd be working hard—cleaning, cooking, taking care of Lucas—and he'd say, "you really should go pamper yourself sometime." But then, when it came down to it, if I ever did go get my nails done or go to the beauty parlor, I knew—I just knew—I was going to come home to a ball of anger and something I'd done wrong. Somehow that sorta took the fun out of it all.

CHAPTER 26

Len (2001)

Now that Lucas has seen Rachel, of course he wants to hang out with us whenever she comes over. And it is not long before I come upon 'the incident.' That's how I think about it in my head, 'cause I can't quite wrap my head around how it even happened. The three of us spend the afternoon wading in the creek, turning over rocks to look for salamanders, and chewing on bright green stalks of marsh grass as we sit beside the creek. I suggest we play tag, but Lucas pulls out his pack of cigarettes instead. Rachel is much cooler than me. She takes one when he offers it to her, puts it in her mouth and lights it as if she does it all the time. So I try it too. It burns my throat when I breathe in, and I cough like a rookie. But I put on a brave face, like it is nothing, and I take another drag. But the honest truth is that after that cigarette, I am starting to feel a little sick to my stomach. I tell them I have to go to the bathroom, and I trudge back to the house, drink a long cool glass of water, and lie down for a few minutes. I feel about back to normal after that, so I head back out to find them again.

The air is quiet, and the sun is hot in the sky. I walk down the dirt pathway to the barn door. The big doors are partway open so I figure maybe they came in for the shade. I walk in, pausing a moment to let my eyes adjust to the dim light, and am just about to call out when I hear muffled noises coming from behind some bales of hay. Cautiously I walk around to see what is there, smelling the hay and sweet feed mixed together. Then I stop, rooted to the spot. Leaning against the hay bales are Rachel and Lucas, arms wrapped around each other. They are kissing, and Lucas makes a funny little moan. I start to leave, when Rachel opens her eyes and sees me. We look at each other for a moment, then she closes her eyes again, and I turn and leave the barn.

I stomp up the stairs to the screen porch and let the door slam behind me. I am almost shaking I am so mad. Why did Lucas even have to come here? And why did I even tell him anything—I should never have introduced him to Rachel.

I am sitting on the screen porch curled up and trying to read my book when Rachel comes up and sits beside me on the wicker sofa. She looks at me, and then looks down at her feet. I keep my nose in my book, but can't concentrate on the words.

"Why were you kissing him?"

She shrugs. "I don't know. He wanted to."

I close my book and look straight at her. "There's this word you can use," I say. "It's called 'no.'"

She rolls her eyes at me. "I don't know, I guess I just felt like it."

I get a funny feeling in the pit of my stomach right then. I don't say anything else. I don't want her to say anything else. I just want to go back to the way we had been before and pretend that I never saw them together.

I am still thinking about it that night. And as I am trying to fall asleep I get this idea. What if I did just run off and find Clifton? Ma and Granny and Walter would get over it—they'd be mad for a while, but they'd get over it. And I'd sure show Rachel and Lucas. I'd show them they can leave me out of things if they want to, because I sure as heck don't need them. So I get out my backpack and I stuff in a few changes of clothes and my extra toothbrush. I'm not planning to leave right then, but I want to be ready. I sneak quietly out the back door and head towards the barn. The moon is bright, and the night air is cool. It whispers to me, telling me I am on the right track. The crickets chirp and the bullfrogs make up a chorus. The world is telling me I am doing the right thing. I stash my bag in the tack room and head back to bed.

CHAPTER 27

Cora (1988)

When she did not start school in the fall, Cora had to explain her presence in town—to her friends, to people she bumped into who knew her and her family. It got easier as time went on, and what started as an embarrassed sort of mumble weeks later turned into a proud statement.

It was the next question that threw her—some form of either "Who's the father?" or "Did you get married?" She became pre-emptive, sometimes saying she had gone to a sperm bank, sometimes making up a story about a fiancé that had been killed in a tragic accident at the tortilla factory. When she was feeling particularly feisty, she'd talk about how she and her girlfriend were living with her mom for now but were saving to get their own place. Abilene was a small town, but no one really seemed to be phased by her stories, so after a while, she just started to tell the truth—the pregnancy wasn't planned and her boyfriend left town without a trace, and she was just thrilled to pieces to be having this baby. The funny thing was, it was the truth that elicited the warmest response—no one ever judged her, and all she ever received was warm support. She'd known the people in this town all her life—since before she'd cut off all her hair and dyed the stubs black. Since before she'd started buying all her clothes at Goodwill and had sworn off wearing any colors, only black and white. They could look past it all. They accepted her just as they accepted her parents with their hippie lifestyle. Her family was simply known as eccentric.

So Cora settled into life on the dairy ranch, while her belly grew. She took on her share of the chores. There were machines for milking, and Walter did most of the labor around the place, hiring day workers when they were needed. But she worked on the garden and helped with the cows. She ordered the textbooks she would have had to buy if she'd gone back to school, promising herself she would read every one and would not slack off on her studies. Maybe she'd just jump right on ahead and write a dissertation—or maybe a book.

Every morning Cora knelt at the flower bed in front of the porch. The air would turn from dew-laden to dry and the midmorning sun warmed her back as she worked. She had an old set of work gloves always with her, but she didn't put them on. She liked the feel of the earth on her skin. She needed to feel it so she knew if the soil was right or not. She couldn't explain how, but she knew from the touch whether a seed would take and sprout, or whether she needed to head out to the massive compost pile with a shovel and wheelbarrow to collect more of the most fertile soil around.

As her garden grew, so did her belly. As the weather turned crisp, she began to notice the extra effort it took to kneel, to bend over, reaching for weeds. So she began to start her plants in pots—always with a murmured apology to Plato. But she was not doing it so they would flower in eight days and then be tossed aside. She did it only to nurture them temporarily, until the roots had started and became strong enough to plant where they would have to compete with roots and insects and animals. And also, of course, so she didn't have to bend at the waist so much.

CHAPTER 28

Granny (1989)

Cora's mother sat in the living room, the window open to the night air, her hands busy weaving a piece of Virginia Creeper vine—twisting it over and over. In front of her on the low table was the small clutch of comfrey mixed with wild senna she had collected a few weeks before, under a moon so bright it cast shadows. She placed the herbs in a tiny sackcloth and twisted the vine around to close it tight. Then she looped a long thread through, so that it dangled like a necklace.

This was before she was "Granny." Back when she was "Mrs. Walker" or "Lorelai" to some. But she remembered— she remembered a time long ago, before she had the children, and before she ever met the man who would be her husband. A time when she had no name.

She had grown up in the back country, where her feet sank in the deep mud of the riverbank while she learned to fish. Her feet in the black earth, squishing, hiding in the willows, she learned to feel through it for the sound of the fox, or the rabbit, so that there would be meat. Her Pa taught her to catch rabbits with a snare set with lettuce and vinegar. They'd skin the rabbit and gut it and then cook it over an open flame. But she liked the porcupines better. The skinning was more difficult, but the meat was fatty and flavorful, and she could sleep all night without the pangs of hunger waking her.

She hadn't learned the sounds of the English language, and for this, people—the few times they ever saw her—thought her slow. On those few occasions she walked with her parents down the long dirt road to the town, she came to understand that those around her did not know what she meant by the signs she made with her hands, or her nuanced grunts and syllables. Once a woman, clean and fresh, stepped in front of her with a smile and made signs of her own. But they made no sense and when Lorilai stood with a blank expression on her face and her parents turned away, the woman had deflated. She heard the sounds around her in town, but she had no one to teach her what they meant. And so she learned to rely on something deeper, something inside that could speak to the willows, to the ripples in the pond and the wind as it lifted the wings of an osprey stretching out its talons.

It was not until her mother made the twelfth mark on the doorway of the old farmhouse that she was taught the meaning of sounds by anyone with two legs. For shortly after that the prim woman with a notebook and the man with large hands had come to take her away. She had not known what was happening. Only that Pa had not come home for two days, and her mother sat in her rocking chair, rocking back and forth and back and forth, even when Lorelai placed a bowl of rabbit stew in her hands and made the signs, telling her to eat it, she had only stared dully ahead of her, her eyes blank.

That was the last image she had of her mother, because she would not get out of the chair when the strangers came for her. She would not look at them or try to convey any meaning with her hands as she sometimes did. But Lorelai would forever remember the cry her mother had uttered as Lorelai left with the strangers. It was low and long and animal—the pain inside it so palpable it was alive. It followed her out the door, and to the car—something she had never been even close to before in her life. Lorelai kept that cry with her, inside of her, as the car rumbled to life, her knuckles white as she gripped the seat. She kept it inside of her as they moved, dreamlike down the lane with mulberry trees she knew every branch of, and onto the paved road that they used to walk along to get to town—her mother on one side of her, soft and warm, and her father on the other, lifting her on his shoulders if she tired of walking. And in her head, she echoed her mother's cry, note for note.

Now, Granny used some of the half-words, some of the sounds her mother had taught her long ago. They had slept within her for these many years, as she grew accustomed to the ways of other people. Her own husband had never even known of the life before, so adept had she been in her camouflage. But she awakened these sounds now, as her daughter lay sleeping. Coralee slept soundly, breathing deep, even breathes. She lay on her side, her belly sticking out towards Granny making it easy for her to hold the amulet over the largest part while she whispered the rhythmic sounds. She pictured the boy, young man, she reminded herself, with his easy smile, his bashful brown eyes, and she felt, she felt so deeply, his love for Cora. She knew it had been there, in the room with them, palpable and present. She did not know where he was or what had happened, but she felt that love and longing and put it all into the little seed that grew in her daughter's womb. This baby would be a beacon, a siren call that could not be ignored. She would keep the despair, the darkness, at bay. This baby would bring her own father home.

CHAPTER 29

Jean (2001)

Jonny is looking at me, the concern clear on his face. "I've been talking to people, doing some digging," he says.

"Okay," I say, waiting for him to tell me more.

"I'll tell you, part of what started me looking into things was when I heard what you told Dr. Scott about that Christmas party you went to, and what you said to Don and Franny Carter."

"You find out what I said that was so horrible?" I ask, wondering what it is that I am finally gonna hear about. He looks so serious, so concerned, that I get nervous. My palms are sweating a little as I lean forward to hear what he has to say.

"Well, look, you know I'm a defense attorney. This is a pretty small town, so when someone gets arrested for something, when someone needs a defense attorney, I usually know about it. Even if that person has money for a private lawyer, even if he doesn't need me, I'll hear about it. Us guys doing this sort of work, we talk."

I nod, wondering where he is going with this.

"Well, let me tell you why I was surprised when Dr. Scott shared your story with me. Don Jr., Don and Franny Carter's son, was arrested for indecent exposure just around the time of that party you mentioned. Now, indecent exposure—that sounds like maybe he was drunk and took a piss in the street or something, but that wasn't it. He'd been caught having sex in the men's bathroom at the bus station—with another man."

I squint at him, slow to understand what that has to do with me.

"The news was all over the place, as you can imagine—this family has money, this kid is a football player and headed for college, and then everyone finds out he's gay. I mean, yes he's arrested too, but in this town that is the least of it. That pales in comparison to being caught being gay. The parents tried to hush things up, but there was only so much they could do. They were able to keep it out of the local papers mostly because they were friends with the editor. But everyone knew anyway."

And I am thinking not so much about the plight of poor Don Jr. and his family, but about what Roger knew, and what he told me.

"So, he didn't get into TCU?" I ask.

Jonny folds his hands in front of him. "Well, he did, initially. Although he ended up at community college instead. But that wasn't news at the time you went to that Christmas party, Jean. What I am telling you is gonna be hard for you to hear. What I'm telling you is that it sounds like Roger set you up. Roger would have known all about Don Jr. He couldn't have predicted exactly what you'd say, but he could be certain that, if he suggested that you to congratulate them because of their son, things would at least be awkward for you."

I feel, for a moment, as if the floor has dropped out from under me as—just like I felt when I was talking to Mabel. I replay the evening in my head, Roger driving to the party and telling me everyone's news. I am certain he said their son had just been accepted into TCU, certain of it. I remember my exact words to Franny and Don. I have replayed the evening so many times in my head over the years, trying to figure out what had gone wrong, that the memory is right there waiting for me. "I heard about your son Don Jr.—congratulations, you must be so proud." Those were my exact words. And now, I can completely understand their reaction.

But I don't just remember that part. I remember, as if it was yesterday, Roger's face as I told him what had happened. I remember him insisting that I must have said something else. I remember his anger at me, his frustration and disappointment.

I remember him making me feel broken, unhinged, and always a failure. And I remember him telling me I smelled bad. I am too stunned to speak.

I'm thinking about all this and watching Jonny as he fidgets and then pulls something out of his briefcase. It is a slim book, and he holds it in front of him for a moment, then takes a deep breath.

"That behavior fits some other things you described to Dr. Scott. She thought this book might help you." He looks at me. "I believe your story Jean. I think there was another woman there, and I don't think you planned this ahead of time. I believe that you just snapped."

He places the book on the table and slides it over to me. He has turned it around so that it arrives in front of me right side up. "Emotional Abuse: How to Recognize the Signs and How to End It."

I don't say anything for a long time. I sit there looking at that title for what feels like hours.

Jonny watches me, his face kind and concerned. "I'm gonna do my best for you, Jean. I've been talking to some people about other instances, other things Roger was doing. I know this is a lot to take in right now. It might be a little overwhelming, but I need to talk to you about how we can use this in your defense. Being subject to abuse—even if it were physical abuse—doesn't give you the right to shoot someone. I can't get you off the hook. But I might be able to get a little leniency."

"But he never hit me," I say. "I wasn't abused."

He looks thoughtful. "Not physically you weren't. He was much more subtle."

"I thought maybe you wanted me to plead insanity?"

He shakes his head. "You don't have the grounds for that. You are just as sane as I am Jean. It's just that Roger's been manipulating you for so long it's made it hard for you to see things clearly."

Funny, but in the middle of all this information, I am so relieved that he doesn't think I'm crazy. I don't even know if

I answer him or not. I am lost and swirling in the title of that book and what it means for the last fifteen years of my life. I am in a daze as I am walked back to my cell. Jonny tells me he got approval for me to keep the book, and so I hold onto it tightly as I walk.

I have known, since I talked to Mabel of course, that Roger has been lying to me about some things. I have known, deep inside I think, for longer than that. But it was never a knowing. It was always a suspecting. And every time, he convinced me that it was me.

It takes me a little while before I have the nerve to open that book. I sit on my hard, lumpy cot, and smooth my hand across the cover. I turn it over and read the blurb on the back, talking about how, often, people in an emotionally abusive relationship don't even know they are being abused. I stare at those three little bullet points, hinting at what is inside:

> • Do they tease you, or use sarcasm as a way to put you down or degrade you?
> • When you complain, do they say that "it was just a joke" and that you are too sensitive?
> •Do you feel you must "get permission" before going somewhere or before making even small decisions?

In my head, I am nodding yes to every one of these.

So I open that book. And when I look at the rest of the list—"30 warning signs" is what it is titled—there are over 20 things on that list that ring absolutely true to me.

I stay up all night reading that book. And every few pages it's like little firecrackers start going off in my head. What hits me hardest is the feeling that I am not alone, that I am not crazy. And in spite of the many times I think to myself—well, Roger wasn't as bad as this guy they're describing here—I know that the stories these women are telling in the pages of this book are so much like my story. There is so much spinning inside me as I read the book. There is relief—relief that I am not crazy, and that there is a name for what's been happening to me. And there is a lot of regret and a lot of anger. How could I not have listened to that voice in my head in the beginning. But every time I thought something was off, he would convince me it was me. Even in the very beginning, back when we were first dating.

I think about how things were in the beginning. How maybe I glossed over some things that I should have been more concerned about. I remember one of those early nights, when it was all new and exciting. There were little things—things that at the time I just passed over, thinking I was just getting used to being in a relationship.

I remember one night, the first night Roger took me out to meet some of his friends. The music had been loud at the Lobo. It was still early, but the regulars were already squinting over their beer and swaying just a bit on their barstools. When Roger put his hand around my waist as he talked to his buddies, I felt a sense of pride. I was his. He was here with me, and he was staking his claim, right out there where everyone could see. I smiled at his friends as he introduced them, and I sipped my beer.

The dance floor was getting crowded. I stood with the other girlfriends, and we chatted for a while. And when they headed off to go to the powder room, Jimmy Sterling leaned in from his barstool to talk to me. He asked me about my job and told me a story about his dog going fishing. I laughed and looked over to catch Roger's eye. He was looking at me, no smile on his face. But I thought, oh, we are having such a good time. Maybe he's thinking that it's nice I can get along with his friends. Isn't that one of the signs you should be with someone—they get along with your friends, and you can see them in your life for a long time? That is what I thought, and I smiled at him and talked with Jimmy for a bit more before I moved over to his side. The other girlfriends had not come back, and I saw them over in the back of the bar behind the dance floor, talking animatedly to each other.

I moved so I was next to Roger, and I boldly put my hand on his arm—to tell him I was there, I was there with him, and he was there with me. But he turned to face me and said, with an edge to his voice, "Are you having a good time?" His eyes were hard and cold, and I knew it was not the innocent question it might sound like to a stranger.

"Sure," I answered after a moment.

"Because it sure looks like you're having a good time to me," he said.

"Sure," I said again, trying to think why he was mad at me, trying to think what could have possibly happened in those twenty minutes we'd been there to make him mad at me. "Your friends are nice."

"Uh huh." He nodded his head as if I had proved whatever point he was trying to make. "Yeah, I can tell you like my friends."

"What's wrong Roger?" I asked, "Are you mad at me or something?"

"Oh no." His voice was nasty and sarcastic. "Oh no. I love it when the girl I bring starts flirting with all my friends."

"What?" I looked at him like he was crazy. "I wasn't flirting. I was just talking to your friends, just trying to be nice."

"Well you sure as hell could have fooled me," he said, and he turned back around to his group, his back to me. So I stood there, not sure what to do, my stomach churning.

The rest of the evening I did not talk to his friends. I stood beside him, forcing a smile when someone talked to me, trying to join in with the other girlfriends when they returned to the group. But the night had turned gray and tasteless. I considered leaving, but Roger drove me there, and I didn't have a way to get home. Also, I thought maybe if I didn't talk to anyone else the rest of the night, he wouldn't be mad at the end. Maybe on the way home he'd apologize for misunderstanding.

But when we got in the car, he was silent and still. The parking lot was loud, with the music spilling out of the doors of the bar, and people shouting goodbyes to each other, but in the car it was quiet. He turned on the engine and pulled out of the parking space. My eyes filled suddenly with tears.

"I'm sorry Roger," I said softly.

And I was sorry. Sorry that what I thought was a wonderful night had been completely ruined. Sorry that we were fighting, and that he was mad because he misunderstood something.

Roger peeled out of the parking lot, drove quickly and silently to my street, and parked a block away. He sat, gripping the wheel, looking down at his hands. "You just have to think about how that looks to other people—like you don't respect me," he said.

"I wasn't flirting Roger, honest."

"Well, it looked like it. It looked like it to everyone in there. And I just wouldn't want all those people to get the wrong idea." His voice was more regular, the hard edge had softened somewhat and he said, "Because I really like you Jean." He turned his head to look at me. "I think I may be falling in love with you." He reached out and put his hand on my cheek. It was warm, and a little electric, and I got a little lost in my thinking. No one had ever made me feel like that before, and when he kissed me, the funny feeling I had in the pit of my stomach melted away and I was lost.

CHAPTER 30

Jean (2001)

I am a bit in a fog for a while after reading that book.

I am thinking of all the times I thought I must be going crazy. I am thinking about all those arguments where I knew I was right—I knew deep inside that he was not being fair, that he was the one in the wrong. But every time, he convinced me it was me.

There is a part of me that knew something was truly messed up early on. But only sometimes. As soon as I would start thinking something was really wrong, Roger would be so thoughtful and kind and wonderful, and I'd put all my worries away in the closet, hoping things would stay good. I buried everything for so long.

I remember when we were first married. That year before Lucas was born. I don't remember the details each time, but I remember that feeling—like I got the wind knocked out of me. But somehow, I always let him convince me. Somehow it was always my fault. My "issues." And somehow, I would just catch my breath and get right back in the game.

We'd been married maybe a month when I got the flu. My whole body ached, my head pounded, and I burned with a fever. Roger brought me some DayQuil and a glass of water. "You gonna be OK?" he asked, his brow furrowed with worry for me.

I smiled up at him. My new husband who loved me. "Sure," I nodded. "I'm just gonna call Billy Joe and tell him I can't come in today. Then all I want to do is sleep."

Roger nodded and stood up. "OK, well call me if you need anything."

"I will." I smiled a weak smile. I blew him a kiss as he headed out the door.

I phoned in to work and let them know I was sick, and then slept for most of the morning. Noonish I dragged my aching self out of bed and forced myself to walk down the stairs to eat a piece of toast and drink some orange juice. As I was coming back upstairs, I heard the phone ring. My head was pounding even when I moved slowly, so I just let it ring. I crawled back into bed and took another nap.

I felt a little better when I woke, and propped myself up in bed and turned on the TV. I was flipping channels—soap opera, The Price is Right, I Love Lucy re-runs—when I heard the door slam downstairs and Roger's heavy steps on the stairs. I looked at the clock—he was three hours early.

As soon as he appeared in the doorway, I could tell he was mad. His jaw was set and his eyes were hard. "Hi honey," I said, a bit of a question in my voice. "How come you're home so early?"

He raised his eyebrows and gave a little huff, as if he couldn't even believe my question. "How come I'm home so early?" it sounded like "how dare you ask me that question." Then he said, "Are you comfortable?" He glanced at the TV. "Get caught up on all your soap operas did you?" His voice was dripping with anger and sarcasm.

I knew he was angry, but I was just lying here sick all day, so it couldn't possibly be me he was angry at. "What's the matter, honey?" I asked. "Did something happen at work?"

Roger laughed. Not a funny laugh, but a mean laugh.

"Yeah, something happened. What happened was you didn't answer the phone and so I worried for the next hour and then I called you again and you didn't answer again."

"Oh - I'm sorry," I said. "I didn't know it was you calling. I didn't get to the phone in time—I thought it was just a telemarketer." I leaned my head back on the pillows and turned the volume down on the TV. "I really felt like shit all day," I said, thinking he would commiserate.

But he pursed his lips into a thin line, nodded at me, went into the bathroom and slammed the door. Before long I heard the shower running. I felt like someone just punched me in the gut. On top of the fact that I was still burning with fever and felt absolutely horrible, I didn't understand why he was so angry at me. And the pit in my stomach stayed there, turning to worry, because I didn't know how to fix it.

So I stayed in bed. I turned off the TV and just leaned my head back on the pillows. After a while the shower turned off, and I could hear Roger rustling around in there. I waited for him to come out, my stomach in knots.

He opened the door with his stone face, walked over to the closet and started to get dressed.

"Roger," I said softly. "Why are you so mad? I'm sorry I didn't answer the phone. I didn't think it was anything—I was just sick and wanted to sleep."

"You didn't think it was anything." He made a face like he was thinking hard about that. "Maybe that's the problem right there. You didn't think about me. About how I might be feeling. That I might be worried about you." He sat down on the bed beside me and ran a hand through his wet hair. "I get worried about you. I just think you need to respect me enough to think about what I'm feeling."

I nodded.

"When you didn't answer, I thought what if she's so sick she slipped into a coma or something. What if she got up to take a shower and slipped and hit her head and she's lying there and can't get to a phone to call 911?"

My stomach relaxed mostly. "I'm sorry Roger." I hadn't thought that he might worry. I could see, when he explained it, how maybe I wasn't being very sensitive to him. I figured I was still getting used to the idea of what it means to be married. I still felt achy and terrible, but I reached out and touched his shoulder. "I just didn't realize."

He nodded. And I could tell the anger was almost gone. "Are you hungry?" I asked. "I could make you something?"

He nodded. "I'm starving. I couldn't eat lunch I was so worried." He looked at me. "Can you make that brisket you promised?"

I had promised to make that brisket he loved before I got the flu. The last thing in the world I felt like doing was standing up for hours in the kitchen. But I offered to make him something, didn't I? He made me feel like I had been so selfish, lying there in bed while he'd been crazy with worry.

"Sure honey," I said. And I pulled back the covers, got up, and spent the rest of the afternoon making his favorite meal. Roger popped open a bag of chips and put the game on while I worked.

But I thought it was all OK. Because he loved me and he cared about me so much that he was worried.

When did I know it was not really OK?

It was such a slow creeping. Did I realize it the next time something happened and I didn't get to the phone and he sulked and wouldn't speak to me for an entire day? Or later, when I left for a hair appointment thinking he would be gone fishing by the time I got back. And then I ran into Gail at the beauty parlor and we decided to go out to lunch. And when I got home, I found him sputtering and angry and accusing me of "sneaking around" and "going off to meet some guy." Each time it was just a tiny bit more of a reaction then the last. And each time he had me so convinced that I was the one who had been insensitive.

So years later I am trained that if the phone rings I am damned sure going to race across the house, put down whatever I am doing in an instant, and answer it. And if I am out on some errand and want to do something else, usually I don't—I just go home. And if I do, I make sure to stop at a pay phone and call Roger—even if he's at work, I call to let him know, because what if he came home early and I wasn't there. And if I can't reach him, I just go home. I spend all my time just trying to keep the peace.

CHAPTER 31

Jean (2001)

The one thing about being here, in this cold dank metal and concrete place, is I sure have time to think. I think about that visit to the doctor who couldn't find anything wrong with me even after he ran all those tests. I remember the concern on his face when we told him about my symptoms. Roger and me. That was who told him. Roger made sure to come to that appointment with me.

And I decide right then and there, I want to make a phone call. There are only certain times a day that you can use the pay phone. And the way they keep the phone calls down to a minimum is that they charge so much per minute that no one in here can sit there chatting for too long. So I have to wait until the afternoon, and then I am allowed to head over to the phones. I look through the tattered phone book—the cover is nearly falling off, its pages torn in places. I find the number of that doctor, and I use the pre-paid calling card that I use when I call Lucas even though he is sullen and sad on the phone.

It takes a little talking to get the doctor on the phone—first he is "not available at the moment." But when I explain who I am and that I am calling from prison to talk to him, he's able to make it to the phone right quick.

I tell him how I have found out Roger lied about certain things, I tell him I am starting to wonder whether I even did have all those symptoms we came and talked to him about. At first he is all business. But after we talk a while, he loses his phone voice.

"Did you ever find anything at all wrong with me?"

"Well, I'm looking through your file as we're talking, and I see we ran diagnostics. We conducted a neurological examination and an EEG. But all of that was inconclusive." After a pause he says, "I remember you and Roger coming in, Jean. Just like I said then, there was—there is, I suppose—a possibility you had early onset Alzheimer's. That's why I suggested that you come back in about six months so we could do further testing. Often the symptoms will increase over time, making a diagnosis easier."

"So Doctor Grady, I just have to ask you—did you see me acting confused or anything like that? Like, if me and Roger hadn't told you about all those problems I was having at home, would you have thought there was something wrong with me?"

There is a pause for a moment. "No, Jean. You seemed just fine to me. But that can happen sometimes. Especially at first. That's why I wanted you to come back later, to see if the disease had progressed."

I nod, but of course he can't see me. "Thanks Dr. Grady. I sure do appreciate you talking to me."

"You're my patient. It's no problem at all."

"Oh—there's one more thing I wanted to ask you—did I smell bad when I came to see you?"

"Excuse me?"

"Well, did I have really bad body odor or anything? Roger used to tell me all the time that I had such strong BO, and I remember it was warm that day we came for the appointment. I was just wondering if you noticed if I smelled bad."

"No. I think you smelled just fine, Jean." His voice sounds a little sad to me when he says that, but maybe I am just imagining it.

I am on a roll now, so I use that messed up phone book again to look up Boyd Sullivan's number. Only after he picks up and I say my name do I realize that this phone call is probably a bad idea.

"What in the hell are you callin' me for?"

How can I really blame him? I would probably have the same reaction if I were in his shoes. I think fast.

"Boyd," I say, "I gotta ask you a question—but it's for Roger. It's not to help me or anything."

"Well damn right I wouldn't help you, bitch." He's been drinking, his words swish around in his mouth just a little.

"Remember that time you came over for dinner? The last time I seen you I guess?"

"Hmm," he grunts. I take it as a yes.

"Remember how I left the room, and when I came back I got all confused because I hadn't remembered eating half my food already? Do you remember that?"

There is a pause and I realize I probably sound more than a little crazy right at the moment. But I keep going. "Did you guys mess with me? I mean, I figure it was just a joke, but I just want to know for sure."

"Jesus, Jean—of course it was a joke. He said you guys would have a good laugh about it later—that you were always pranking each other."

I am silent. I'm not surprised, just a little stunned. All this time.

"I had a hard time keeping a straight face through all that." He is definitely drunk, no question now. "What the hell are you calling me for anyway, Jean?"

"Thanks Boyd," I say as I hang up. I am in a bit of a trance as I stand, my hand on the phone until someone yells at me to move my ass so she can use it.

I read that book again before lights out that night, read it cover to cover. And I spend the night wondering about almost every interaction I have had in the past fifteen years. It is like I have two different movie screens in my head looking back on my life. One shows me crazy as hell and the other shows me putting up with the most messed up shit I can imagine—one of them ladies pushed around so much she just learned to take it and shut up. I don't feel like either one of those people is me. I don't know what is me and what is not. I don't know what is real anymore.

CHAPTER 32

Len (2001)

When Ma calls me in to her study, she looks a little frantic, like maybe she is freaking out just a little bit. I know right away what she wants to talk to me about.

"Len—why would you send this email? I wasn't ready...I wasn't even sure I wanted to send it. And it was my email—it should have been up to me."

I look down at my feet.

"Well I got a response," Ma says. "And it does not look like we'll be seeing your father anytime soon."

"What does it say?"

Ma shakes her head. "Nothing. Nothing at all."

I move so I can look over her shoulder. "Thank you for your correspondence. Mr. Wilkes regrets that he is unable to answer your message personally." There is a link to his website, some fan club information, and not much else.

My heart is beating fast. The email is totally lame, but even so, I feel like there is progress, like we are getting closer. "I saw his concert schedule," I say. "He's playing Houston on Friday, and then Dallas and Austin after that."

"Yeah, looks like he hit the big time." Ma sounds a little bitter, but I ignore it.

"Well, I think we should go," I say. "I mean, now that he's all famous and stuff, how are we ever gonna be able to even talk to him unless we just walk right up to him?"

"No," she says, her face pinched. "I'm not putting us through that. If he doesn't want to see us, we can't make him."

It is so unfair. I can feel the unfairness down to the tips of my fingers. "You think he won't want to know about me don't you? You think I'd just be a mistake to him too."

"What are you talking about?"

"I heard you. You don't have to pretend anymore—I know you just think I've been a burden to you."

"What on earth? Why would you say something like that?"

"I heard you," I repeat. My face is twisted, I am trying not to cry. "I heard you tell Bo I was a mistake. Well, I'm so sorry to have ruined your life and all—but it's not like I actually had a say in the matter."

"What? I've never said anything like that."

"Yes you did. Saturday when we got back."

She thinks about it.

"Oh Len," Ma looks deflated. "I wasn't saying you were a mistake. That's not at all what I meant." She pats her knee like she wants me to sit in her lap, but I make my way to the couch and sit there instead, facing her desk chair.

"I was young when I met your father, you already know that. But I don't suppose you know the rest." She sighs and presses her fingers together in her lap. "I thought I knew everything when I was young. I thought I was so tough." She gets up and moves over to sit beside me on the couch. "I loved him Len. I loved him in a way you can probably only love someone when you are young like that. And my mistake was in thinking that he loved me too. I was wrong, I guess. I know, it is surprising, but sometimes I can actually be wrong." She laughs a little and glances over at me. I try not to smile.

"I thought what we had was some earth shattering, world changing kismet," Ma says. "But the honest to God truth is that he just up and left town one day without even saying goodbye to me. And that is really all there is to it. Just a case of me thinking this was a love story, and it was really just a fling. That was my mistake. Being a sucker, being gullible. But not you. You were like the Christmas present under the tree that I had no idea I wanted so much. You were the most special gift, and I would never change a thing about what happened, because it gave me you."

I look down at my hands. "I thought that I was the mistake," I say softly.

"No, Baby," Ma says. "You are my crowning achievement."

When Ma reaches over to hug me, I let her.

CHAPTER 33

Len (2001)

I am still mad at Rachel. I am hurt still, and I wish she'd never even met my cousin. But I also keep thinking about that bag I packed sitting in the hayloft, and I keep thinking that if Rachel came with me, I would definitely have the guts to take that bag and go. Without her I'm not sure I can bring myself to do it. So the next day I head over to her house, and I plan to have it out with her.

"We need to talk," I say when Rachel answers the door.

"Not here," she says, nodding towards the hallway so I know she doesn't want her mom to hear she's been kissing a boy. "Ma, can you drive us over to the pool?" she calls out.

I stand in the hall with Rachel and wait. Soon Mrs. Corbin arrives, jingling her keys and holding onto a massive purse. Her polyester thighs make a soft swishing noise as she walks down the hall. She is having a good day.

"Do you girls need a snack before you go?"

Rachel rolls her eyes. "No Mom, we're good."

We walk out the front door and into the heat.

Right then is when everything goes green. So green I can barely see in front of me. But I can hear—so I know someone is parking a car, getting out and roughly slamming the door. I stand still and move my head around trying to see, but it's like when you have your eyes closed and there is a bright light in front of you and all you can see is the color of the insides of your eyelids. It's sort of like that, mostly greenish. But I can feel the stillness of the air, the change in the heartbeats of the people around me. And I can tell from the roughness of the footsteps on gravel that a man is walking from the car towards us.

"Where are ya'll headed?"

There is silence on our end.

"It's a nice place you got out here. Prettier than Lubbock, that's for sure."

I can feel Mrs. Corbin shift beside me. "It's not your weekend," she says finally, her voice strained.

"Wasn't easy to find you neither." I hear the steps coming closer. "Almost felt like you were hiding or something—almost felt like you didn't want me to find you."

"You're not supposed to come to the house. The McDonalds on South Street, that's what the Court Order says."

Then, two things happen at the exact same time. I hear the crunch of wheels at the far end of the driveway—a car turning in from the main road, and I feel Mrs. Corbin and Rachel both breathing again beside me. It's like someone took a pin and popped a balloon down near where you tie it—real quiet like—no big bang or anything but the air just quietly goes out.

"Looks like you got company. You got a boyfriend or something?" Then a gruff laugh. "That's hard to imagine— you must have gained another ten pounds just since I saw you last."

But his voice is moving back, just a little, as the tires get closer. I am blinking like a frog in bright sunlight, but all there is, is green.

"Hi Doris!" It's my mother's voice that calls out when the car door opens. "Hope you don't mind—I just came to pick up Len. I didn't want her walking home by herself in this heat."

I don't know why she came to pick me up when I'd only just gotten here, but I don't say anything.

Ma doesn't say anything else, but I can picture her clear as day, standing there with her skinny arms crossed, just waiting.

"You ain't gonna keep me from seeing my daughter," the voice says. But he sounds like he is heading back to his car.

"I don't have to—the court's already done that." Mrs. Corbin's voice is quiet, but it is firm.

He snorts. "Yeah, I'd like to see that old judge get in my way—all you got is a piece of paper. That ain't shit."

The car door opens. "Don't you worry—I'll be back."

The car starts, and I hear wheels on the gravel again. Around me there are movements, voices blurred somehow like my vision. I hear a dull murmur for a while, and then my hearing comes back, sharply and in focus.

"You call me Doris, day or night." It is Ma's voice talking. I turn my head, with my unseeing eyes toward the voices, putting my arms out, trying to feel for something, and I grab hold of the porch railing and feel my way along it.

I hear my mother sigh. "Len, please. We don't have time for games."

"I'm not playin around, Ma," I say. "I can't see anything— all I see is green."

When I tell her that, she takes me seriously. She puts her hand on my shoulder and guides me to the porch steps. But when I turn back toward the house she says, "Just say goodbye and let's get you in the car."

My vision is beginning to clear, and I blink up at her, still holding onto the railing. "Why? Rach and I were going to the pool."

"Change of plans," she says firmly, and guides me down the steps and into the car.

Her mouth is set firm while she drives out of the driveway. During the short trip my vision clears, and the fuzzy feeling in my head goes away.

Ma parks the car and there, right in front of us in the driveway, is the bag I had stashed in the barn. Neither of us move to get out.

"Walter found your bag in the barn. He thought you'd left it there by accident."

I am silent.

"You want to tell me what it was doing there?"

I narrow my eyes, trying to think of an excuse. Or at least a snappy comeback. Nothing springs to mind.

"Were you planning on going somewhere?"

I shrug.

"Because running away is not the answer here."

I take a deep breath and borrow Rachel's line. "Going to find my father is not the same thing as running away."

"Well actually honey, yes it is."

"Don't you think I deserve the chance to meet him?" The unfairness of it all sits right in the pit of my stomach. "Don't you think at least I deserve that chance?"

Something in Ma softens, and she gets out of the car and comes around to open my door for me. I just sit there. I don't make any move to get out.

"Well this really sucks," Ma says. She walks over to my bag and picks it up. "Because I had already decided we should take a road trip to his concert in Houston."

My eyes widen. "Really?" I can't help it, I break out into a big ole smile.

"But then I find this, and I don't want you to think I'm giving in to this type of behavior."

"You're not giving in Ma," I say quickly. "I would never have actually done it anyway. I packed that bag when I was mad because I thought you said I was a mistake." I am still processing this turn of events. "Really, we're going to Houston?"

She nods. "I guess it's about time isn't it?"

We spend the afternoon getting ready. Ma writes out a list of detailed instructions about how and when to water the plants; she walks the barn and paddock with Walter, going through all the things to be done while we're gone. It is like some floodgate has been opened—like Ma has been sitting still for the past twelve years and all of a sudden she kicks it into high gear. She tells Walter he's in charge of everything on the ranch, calls Bo to make sure he will drop in to check on Granny, and she leaves detailed instructions for everything she can think of. She is suddenly the General organizing our march.

When I head out to the stable to grain the horses that evening, I do it slowly. The air is dry and beginning to cool, as the sky becomes a dull orange. I open the galvanized trash can that holds the sweet feed and scoop a full can out, the sticky smell close and warm. I hear Walter whistling in the tack room as he sweeps up after the day. He does not have to stay this late, I know this. He is done with his work before supper time since I am the one with the evening chores. But I know also that since Ethyl died, he stays later and later. Why would he want to go home to that empty house, where the ghost of her waits in the single dish, sitting in the drying rack, in the side of the bed that stays fresh and unwrinkled.

Granny offered him the guest room in our house after it happened. But he wouldn't take it, wouldn't leave that emptiness of the home he shared with her because it is the emptiness that now reminds him of her, keeps her alive for him. Ma calls me a stable rat in the summer, and I reckon I pretty much am, but up until Rachel came along, Walter was pretty much my best friend. It was Walter who taught me how to string a bow and bend it so the arrow flew straight to the center of the target in the tree. It was Walter who showed me how to put a worm on the hook so that fish would bite.

I was the one to tell Walter about Ethyl. I told him even before it happened. I didn't have that long a warning, but I knew, one day as we mucked the stalls. I could feel the catch in her heartbeat, feel how hard it was for her to breathe. "You have to go home right now!" I yelled at him, as I stood in the stall gasping for breath. And he knew me well enough not to hesitate. He was quicker than I'd ever seen him, but still it had not been enough. I don't ever get the gift in enough time to change anything. So, really it hardly makes sense to call it a gift.

Now, as I finish giving the horses their grain, as I hear their lips wrestle against the wooden bin for the last bits, I head into the tack room to tell him our plan. I realize as I tell him, and he nods slowly, the corners of his mouth turned down as he listens, that it is not much of a plan. I can tell he is a little worried for me. A little worried we might not get the best result from this situation, but he smiles and clasps me on the shoulder, the warmth of his hand staying with me as I head back to the house to re-pack my things.

CHAPTER 34

Len (2001)

The next morning Ma tells me Rachel and her mom are coming with us. When they show up and I see Mrs. Corbin's face, with the red marks stretching to purple across the side of her face, I understand why. Funny, one of us is running toward a father and the other is running away.

My bags are in the car, and Ma is watering the begonias that are already overflowing their baskets along the front porch one last time when Bo and Cisley arrive to pick up Lucas. Lucas comes out of the house with his PlayStation in his hands and a bag slung over his shoulder. He doesn't look at Rachel as he says goodbye to Ma and waves to me. Bo comes over and musses up my hair as if I'm a little kid. I smile and duck away from him. "Listen Squirt," he says, "whatever happens out there, we'll be right here for you when you get back, Okay?"

I nod. "Okay," I say. And he wraps me in a big hug.

When he lets go, I notice Cisley is standing beside him, making little steps almost like she has to go to the bathroom.

"I made something for you Len," she says, holding out what looks like a pair of jeans folded up. "I worked on it all night as soon as I heard where ya'll are going."

I reach out to take the bundle and unfold the fabric.

"Oh, I hope you like it, honey." Her face is anxious, and beneath her pink lipstick and clumped mascara she looks like a little girl.

Everyone is quiet as I hold up a denim jean jacket that sparkles with so many rhinestones it almost hurts to look directly at it. I raise my eyebrows, a bit in shock looking at that thing.

"I just figured you'd need something to wear to that concert. So I got out my Bedazzler," she says. "'Cause I know that it's what you're like on the inside that really counts, but people don't see your insides right away do they? Sometimes they've gotta make a snap decision about you just from what they see on the outside." She reaches out and touches the rhinestones at the collar. "I just want your Daddy to see right away that you sparkle."

We all stare at that thing in silence, and I see Cisley's face, upturned and hopeful.

So I smile and say "I love it Cisley, thank you so much!" and I give her a hug and smell her peppermint chewing gum.

She turns back to Bo and smiles. He grabs her hand and squeezes it, and they walk back to their car and drive away with Lucas in the back seat.

Granny says goodbye to us on the front porch. Her boney hands are cold on my cheeks as she examines my face like she is looking for something. "You take care of yourself, Len," she says, sounding like we are going to be gone for weeks, and she presses a small satchel into my hand and nods at me. I know it is for luck, and I know what I am supposed to do with it.

We put our bags in the trunk, and Rachel and I sit in the back seat while Mrs. Corbin hoists herself heavily into the front. There is a bag filled with Cheetos and M&M's and all sorts of junk food that Mrs. Corbin stuck on the back-seat floor. We turn down the gravel driveway, Ma's face set hard, her eyes straight ahead. We are all going off to battle, and we have no idea what we are in for.

CHAPTER 35
Cora (2001)

C ora sets both hands firmly on the wheel and drives. She lets the miles wash over her, oblivious to the low talk of the girls in the back seat, the heavy periodic breathing from Doris in the seat beside her. The other cars become a blur, the world outside her window becomes a blur, and she just drives. As if there is nothing else except her getting to Edison.

She doesn't know exactly what she is going to say to him. She really—and it pains her most deeply to think of this—does not know if he will even remember her. Sure, he'll most likely remember who she was, that chick he had a fling with when he was in Abilene. But would he really remember? He won't remember it the same way she does, that's pretty obvious. It wasn't the same for him, it couldn't have been the same for him, or he would never have left the way he did.

She remembers all those years on her own. She had taken to gardening right after she became pregnant—there was something about the feel of the earth in her hands, the connection to something primal, that comforted her. Cora would turn over the soil in the flower bed every morning, rubbing it with her fingers to determine whether it needed something-- water, fertilizer, more sunlight. And every season she would plant something new. For she had found that it brought her comfort to always put something in the garden that did not belong. She placed a single purple tulip in the center of a tomato patch, a random handful of squash among the lilies, a row of spinach in the rose bed. It was a bit of irony, an inside joke, a middle finger to the natural order of things.

For she knew she was out of place in the natural order. The mother, the father and the baby. It was what she saw everywhere around her. And what Len saw as well, when she was little at least. Every time Len would ask, her voice full of innocent curiosity, "Where's my daddy?" it was like a knife twisting in Cora's gut. There were always happy families to see—dads on display. They would see them at the park, at the playground, dads dropping off their kids at school, dads dressed in ties to attend preschool graduations, dance recitals, and Daddy-Daughter dances. In her heart Cora told her daughter every day how sorry she was.

The hotel looks dingy even from a distance, one of the letters of the electric sign blinking sporadically, but she pulls in and parks, and everyone spills out stretching and groaning. It is almost six o'clock and the concert starts at eight. Cora really should have been at the venue hours ago. It will be a madhouse now. But then again, how big a star is he really? He's still 'up and coming' so maybe she'll get lucky and there won't be much of a crowd.

She smiles to herself remembering her friend Jane from her Georgetown days. All it took from her was a smile and a flirty opening, and the backstage passes would appear from nowhere, or the door would open and the hefty bouncer would move aside with a smile. It was a gift her friend had, and Cora tries to summon it now. But youth carries with it a coolness that can't be faked. It was the coolness coupled with being pretty that had gotten them in—one without the other wouldn't have done it. But Cora knows that now she isn't either of those things. She is a mom, with stretch marks and crinkles at the corners of her eyes. She wonders again how he ended up singing country music. It's not how she pictured he'd end up. But then again, it is more like the picture than if he had become an accountant. Or an architect. He was an entertainer. There was no doubt he was always that.

Cora pays the lady at the reception desk, waving away Doris' offer of cash. She doesn't mind sharing a bed to save a little money, and she knows if they get more than one room Doris will not let her pay the bill.

"Okay, you all need to stay here while I go do something," she says once they are settled.

The look on Len's face is something she should have anticipated. "Um, I don't think so Cora," Len says.

"Don't call me Cora." But she can't hide the tiredness in her voice. It's not that she doesn't want Len to see Edison. It's not that she wants to keep this experience from her. It's just that she can't trust herself to keep it together when she sees him, when she tells him about Len. That is what she has done all this time, all these years—kept it together. And it strikes her that it would sure be a shame if that all came to an end about now.

"Let's go have a look at the pool, honey," Doris says to Rachel. They move quickly out the door in an obvious effort to give Cora and Len a moment alone. It would truly take all of about two seconds to look at the postage-stamp sized pool they had already seen when they drove into the parking lot.

Cora opens her mouth, hesitating, but when she looks at her daughter, she can tell that Len knows exactly what she is feeling, in that strange, uncanny way of hers. Cora does not need to explain, does not need to say a thing. Len sits down on the side of the bed, her shoulders slumping a little.

"I can feel your sadness Ma, but there's no need for it. He's my daddy—you know it just as well as I do."

Yes, Cora thinks, *but what if he doesn't want to be?* That is the question she will never utter in front of Len, and she tries to push it out of her thoughts now. She's never sure whether Len can actually hear what she is thinking.

"What if I come along but I just wait in the car?" Len asks. But Cora can see that Len is resigned now, something has shifted. And when Cora shakes her head and kisses Len on the cheek, Len lets her go alone without an argument.

It turns out to be a good thing too, because the during the drive to the venue, she relives that summer again in her mind. As Len had grown, every once in a while, Cora would see something in her that would remind her of Edison. The small dimple in her cheek that came out when she smiled, the way she turned her head when she asked a question. It had pained her every time.

Over the years, there was no one else truly important. She never fell again. Never even seriously dated again. There were a few men she dated over the years, a very few that she slept with, all with uninspiring results. There was the grad student who spent the summer in town studying insects. He was cute and intelligent, and they had fun. But he wanted to look so deeply into her eyes when they made love that she found it unnerving. It all seemed sweet and earnest at first, but the prolonged state ended up just being weird, especially at such close quarters it almost made her cross-eyed. She had to pretend to be in the throes of passion just so she could close her eyes and get away from the intensity of his gaze.

Then there was her friend Darla's cousin who came to visit and prompted her to drink way too many tequila shots. She thought 'what the heck' since he was heading out of town the next day, why not have a little fun. But then, when it came right down to it, she was just glad when it was all over and she crept out of bed and found her way home.

She never technically slept with that graphic designer who moved into town and then moved away six months later—she had actually liked him and so she didn't want to jump into bed with him too early. But when she told him that, he took her hand, stuck it in his pants and effectively made her give him a hand job. And although it was just a hand job, she felt violated. What she had not been ready for was not the physical act of sex itself, it was the intimacy of the experience with someone else. When he forced her into that intimacy, she'd felt violated in a way she'd never expected.

Sometimes she'd write Edison letters, knowing she would never send them. If she was in a particularly sappy mood, she would look back at the things she'd written, the journal she kept during that brief moment in time when she believed the world had opened up to her in all its possibilities. The entries were the kind that you look back on later in life with equal parts longing and cringing. Pretentious, intentionally and overtly intellectual, and generously peppered with quotes of things like Sonnet 116. Bits and pieces of her former life that made her both wish for that time again and glad she was past it in equal measure.

She realized eventually, that first love is like a Tsunami. You have no idea what is coming. The air is warm and the wind light, the water pulls gently back from the beach, leaving fish and crabs and mussels displayed like jewels for you to gather in buckets, bring back and feast joyfully upon with no worry as to where the second meal is coming from. But then, eventually, comes the moment when you look up and see the dark wave poised, and in that soul crushing moment you feel the utter and complete devastation that wave will bring, and it crashes down on you, sucking the air out of your lungs and annihilating your entire world. And you will never again feel the same complete and utter abandonment in gathering fish, because there is always a part of you that remains aware, that waits in dread for the next Tsunami.

Cora is glad Len let her come alone, because soon the floodgates open, and what begins as a few small tears trickling down her cheeks ends up as an air-gasping sob fest that forces her to pull over to the side of the road. When it has passed, she dabs at her eyes with the single sad tissue she is able to extract from the bottom of her purse. But she knows there is really nothing to be done about her puffy eyes and red nose. She has one of those faces that does not hide when it has been crying.

By the time she gets to the parking lot, she knows she's too late. She was trying to catch him before the concert started, but she can see by the crowds flocking into the place that she is too late. He might not be on stage yet, but he would certainly be getting ready. She could wait until the concert is over and try her chances waiting by the back door. But that will be the same exact time the screaming girl fans will be there, trying to show off their cleavage to get past the bouncer. She'll just need to come back tomorrow.

Cora sits in the car, the engine off, and tries to tamp down the excitement she feels at his nearness. She reminds herself she should not be acting like some groupy who would do anything to meet the star they are smitten with. She has the ultimate reason to talk to Edison. If anyone is entitled to speak to the guy, it is her.

It is while she is sitting there, wondering whether to just go talk to the bouncer backstage after all, that she sees the bus. It's off by itself in the parking lot behind the venue. A big tour bus with blacked out windows. But from where she sits, it looks like there are lights on inside.

She debates. But really, ultimately, what does she have to lose? She steps out of her car, into the muggy summer night air, and walks to the bus at the far end of the parking lot. The first time she knocks on the door there is no response. The second time, a woman peeks through the curtains and shakes her head. But Cora knocks again, and stands solid, with her hand on her hip, as if there is nothing in this world that will make her move. After one more solid knock, the woman lowers the window and says, "You need to go away or I'll call security."

"Are you his wife?" Cora did not mean for that to be the first thing she said to this woman—but that was what came out. "Girlfriend?"

"That's really none of your business."

But Cora knows now that it was a streak of brilliance to lead with that line, because what better way to get someone asking questions of her than making them jealous?

"Did you know he has a daughter?" Again, not exactly the way she had played out the conversation in her head on the way there. But then again, it wasn't him she was talking to, so the rules had changed.

"And you are so desperate to talk to him that you have to try to sneak into his trailer? Sorry—nice try though."

Cora shrugs. "I'm going to bring her with me tomorrow. Early, before the show. Edison will be just as surprised as you are."

She turns and walks back to her car.

CHAPTER 36

Jean (2001)

I run my fingers across the bars of my cell. The metal is cold and solid. It is almost visiting time, and I am waiting. When the guard comes to let us out, and I shuffle along the hallway with the other girls, for the first time, I feel it. I truly understand that I am trapped here. For the first time, I understand that here, I am constrained. Because the really messed up part of this whole experience is that I have felt more free in here then I have in fifteen years. I don't have to run the entire house to get to the phone so if it's Roger calling he doesn't accuse me of going out somewhere and lying about it. I don't have to make sure to mention all the errands I have to do so he knows how long I will be gone, and to keep my receipts in case he gets it in his head that maybe I pretended I was shopping. And more important than anything else, I have learned that I am not going crazy—I am not losing it. That is hard for me to remember, but I keep reminding myself. I know it's not an excuse for using that gun—but I also know I had to get away from him.

It sounds ridiculous when I think about it. But it sneaks up on you when you live it. I think about that frog in my seventh-grade science class. The teacher put him in a pail of hot water and he jumped right out. But she put him in a pail of room temperature water and turned the heat on real slow. Heated it up like a nice bath. It was so gradual, that frog didn't even notice. Just sort of looked like he gave up and went to sleep just before the water boiled. How could I not have noticed? How could I not have just jumped out? I have always been strong. I have always been independent. I have always pulled my own weight and made my own way. It never seemed possible to me that I would be turned into one of those women. I wouldn't stand for "abuse." I wouldn't.

But then again, here I am.

Ma is already sitting at the table in the visiting room we know too well by now, her eyes tired. I sit down facing her.

"So it's tomorrow, huh?" This is not really a question; we are both very aware that the preliminary hearing is tomorrow.

I nod. I have not yet told her about the book Jonny gave me.

"Ma, I'm not sure I should have gotten married."

She purses her lips together, thinking. "Well, it's not always a bed of roses. Marriage can be hard."

"That's what they always say. But really, it shouldn't be so hard that it's sucking your entire soul dry, should it?"

"I guess not." She shrugs. "It changed you. Once you got married."

"What do you mean?"

She shrugs and looks away. "How long is it going to take, this hearing?"

"It did change me, Ma. You are right about that." I watch her. Finally, I show her the book. I have been holding it under the table as we talk.

She wrinkles her forehead. "Did he hit you, Jean?" Her eyes fill with tears as she asks.

That word 'abuse' stands out, and I know that like me she's only ever known it to mean hitting. I shake my head. And I try to explain. It is not easy to do, but I do the best I can. I know there are more questions, I know it is a lot to take in.

I do remember, years ago, her asking me if everything was okay, asking if I was happy married to Roger. And I remember saying yes. I remember telling myself I was happy, because he loved me and cared about me, and it is never perfect in a relationship anyway. Everyone always talks about how you have to work at marriage. A good marriage takes work. So I said yes, everything is fine. And I smiled and I went on about my life. By the time I might not have answered the same way, I didn't see Ma much anymore, so I never had to answer the question.

She is quiet for a bit, thinking. "Do you realize that anytime I came over to visit, he would find something that you had to do right then? Some reason you couldn't just sit and visit with me? It made me feel unwelcome, and I just stopped coming by so much." She purses her lips together. "And you got jumpy— seemed like you were always looking over your shoulder. You couldn't even make plans to meet for lunch without checking with Roger—even if he was gonna be at work so why would he care? So no, I didn't know about any 'emotional abuse' like they call it, but I felt a bit like something wasn't right."

She is quiet for a while.

"I'm sorry honey," she says eventually. "I am so sorry I didn't know."

"Me too," I say. "And I mean me, not you. I am so sorry I didn't know either."

CHAPTER 37

Len (2001)

The hotel room smells vaguely of feet. Ma is propped up in bed with her reading glasses on and the spiral writing notebook she takes with her everywhere in front of her. She's even got some massive book by someone whose name I can't pronounce beside her, and I know she is working on that "dissertation" she's been working on forever, probably just so she doesn't have to think about the waiting. Mrs. Corbin is in the bathroom, and I hear the shower. We are all just waiting until it's late enough to go to the concert hall.

The pool here is a joke, but there is absolutely nothing else to do, so Rachel and I spend the day beside it. Rachel lays her towel fussily on the lounge chair and adjusts the straps on her bikini top before sitting down and putting suntan lotion on. Our flip flops are tossed beside our chairs, and we lounge, baking in the sun. I have a book, and Rachel mostly listens to music, the tinny sound drifting over to me once in while.

After a while Rachel sits up, squinting at me with a hand over her eyes like a visor. "I think we should just go on over there now," she says, "to the stadium."

I shrug. "Ma says he won't even be there until later on, before the show."

"How will we know unless we try?" She checks her tan line, then reaches over and changes the station on the small boombox beside her.

I don't notice the boy right away. The first thing I notice is Rachel turning in her chair and standing up. There is a normal kind of standing up to readjust the towel covering a lounge chair, and then there is the kind of standing up so that the boy across the pool can watch you adjust your towel. This is definitely the latter. She holds her stomach in and puffs her chest out the whole time, and makes sure to turn so he has a nice view all around. I almost laugh watching her.

There is a new electricity in the air after that. I can feel it, charged and reverberating. And when I come back from the bathroom the guy is standing by her chair, one hand raised to shield his eyes from the sun, talking to her.

I sit myself down with my book, trying to ignore him. When he finally leaves, Rachel turns to me. "Do you think he's cute?"

I shrug. "Not really."

"I think he's kind of cute. He has nice eyes."

"He looks pretty old to me."

"He's fifteen. That's only a year and a half older than me— that's no big deal."

"I don't know," I say, "he still seems old to me. He's got that little mustache thing even." I make a face and shudder. It is really just a bit of fuzz on his upper lip, but I don't like it.

Instead of being mad, Rachel laughs. "Yeah," she says. "Well, you're right about that."

We get hungry, but before we head back to the hotel room, Rachel wants to make a call. I have a whole lot of things on my mind. And so, when we amble over to the pay phone together and she starts making a call, I am not really paying too much attention. It is only after she starts talking to her dad that I realize what she's doing. I watch her long black hair fall against her face, and I shake my head "no" at her—no, she should not tell him he can come pick her up, no she should not be telling him where we are staying, what hotel, what room number. But she doesn't pay me any mind.

I wonder why she is doing this. Perhaps because things are quiet. And probably a little tense. And maybe she got to feeling like it wasn't all about her and so she just needed a little drama. I know that is what Granny is talking about when she calls Rachel a 'bad influence.'

I try to send her a message without talking, try to let her see with her own eyes how beautiful she is, so she will not need anyone else to tell her. I concentrate hard, willing her to see that she is enough. She does not realize it—she feels she has to be seen by someone else, has to be loved by someone else or she is nothing. But she is enough, all by herself, without any other person to validate her.

But she doesn't seem to be receiving the message I am trying to send, and I don't have the words to make her understand. It gnaws at me, this phone call, as we walk back to the room.

Ma is on the phone, which sounds like maybe a deaf person stayed here last and had the volume up so high. I can hear a woman's voice on the other end, "Oh, we all just love Clifton don't we? You wouldn't believe the things I see girls do just to get a chance to talk to him."

"No," Ma says. "It is not like that. I really need to speak with him about something. It's important."

There is a bit of a laugh on the other end of the phone, and then "I'm so sorry, Ma'am. Even if I wanted to, I can't help you. I'm just running the fan club. It's not like I have any access to Clifton. I met him once at a photo op. I don't have any way to reach him. You'd probably need to get in touch with his manager or something."

Ma asks for his manager's contact information, but of course the chirpy lady doesn't have that. So she hangs up, looking a little downcast.

"It's alright," I tell her. "We'll see him tonight. I'm sure we'll see him tonight."

CHAPTER 38

Jean (2001)

Before we go inside the court room, Jonny reminds me this is not a trial. This is just a preliminary hearing, where the judge decides whether there is enough evidence to hold me for a trial. But even I know they have enough, given I was holding the gun when the police got to the scene, and the fact that I nodded and said yes when that officer asked me if I shot him. Given all that, it's hard to imagine a scenario where there wouldn't be enough evidence to hold me for trial.

The courtroom is not like the ones you see on TV. It's not all plush and dark wood and fancy looking. It looks outdated, with brownish-orange walls, low chairs and worn carpet. The Judge sits on an elevated bench, to his right is a witness stand, and beside that, lined up at right angles, are twelve empty chairs behind a handrail.

The morning goes pretty much like Jonny told me it would. The prosecution calls the officers who arrived at the scene and saw me standing there, the pistol in my hand. They call in the policeman I spoke to right after, and he tells how I looked dazed, staring into space, and how when he asked if I shot Roger I looked right at him and said yes. They call the doctor who examined Roger and operated on him at the hospital. They even drag Buck Chaney in to describe how I came to his shop that afternoon to pick up Roger's gun, and he says how it wasn't Roger that dropped it off there to get fixed either, it was me. And it's all true. He's not lying. He talks slow and looks down most of the time. The one time he does look at me his eyes get all puppy dog-like, so I know he's sorry. I know he doesn't want to be there, but what can he do?

We break for lunch and instead of going back to my cell, I get to sit with Jonny in a room to the side of the courtroom and his secretary brings us sandwiches.

"I'm gonna be putting some people on the stand," Jonny says. "No one's gonna say you didn't shoot him. No one is gonna get you off the hook for that, but I want to show the judge what you've been going through. I want to show him how Roger made you think you were crazy—how difficult he made life for you. It won't get you off—it's not truly a legal defense. But it is what they call extenuating circumstances. If we do it right, it can mean a lesser sentence if they find you guilty later on at a trial. And if we are really lucky, it might convince the prosecutor to drop the charges down from attempted murder one."

CHAPTER 39

Jean (2001)

After the lunch break, it is Jonny's turn. I am thinking this is going to go pretty quick, cause really, whatever that book says, the man never hit me. He didn't even yell that often. When he was mean, it was most often a quiet, sarcastic kind of mean. Or silent. Roger could give me the silent treatment for days. Sometimes so long I couldn't even remember what I was apologizing for. Because it was always me that gave up and apologized just to keep the peace.

I know Jonny's got people lined up to testify and all. But I still can't see as how it's gonna do me much good.

Jonny calls a lady to the witness stand who I have never seen before. She sits down nervously, looking around as if she isn't quite sure either, why she's there.

"Ms. Olson, you're employed as a receptionist in Dr. Grady's office, correct?"

"Yes."

"Were you working on March 14th of last year?"

"Yes, I was."

"How can you be certain?"

"Well, I looked back at my calendar when you called and asked me about it. I always keep my schedule on my calendar because my sister and me, we care for my mama, so we have to make sure our schedules match up right."

"Did Mrs. Goodson ever call you to reschedule her appointment?"

"No sir, I already told you–"

Jonny smiles at the lady and smiles an apology to the Judge. "Ms. Olson, I know that you and I have already discussed these issues, but right now I need you to tell the story so that the judge can hear it."

She swallows and looks nervous again. "Okay."

"Did Mrs. Goodson ever call you to reschedule her appointment?"

"No Sir."

"Then why was her appointment rescheduled?"

"Well, her husband called to reschedule it."

"Could you tell us how that conversation went?"

"Well, the first thing he said was, he asked me if I was working the next day—that's actually why I remember it—cause the first thing he said when I answered the phone is—'are you working tomorrow?' And at first I thought it must be someone I know so I said 'who is this?' and he says, 'I'm calling to reschedule an appointment, are you working tomorrow?' And I say 'no, tomorrow is my day off.' So he says 'well my wife has an appointment tomorrow and I need to reschedule it—can she come in the day after tomorrow?' So I look in the book and I say sure, that would be fine and I book her appointment."

"And then, you wrote down—'patient called to reschedule'?"

"Yes."

"Why did you write that down?"

"He asked me to. He said sometimes his wife gets confused, and in case she came in the next day, since I wouldn't be there, that note would be there and it would help her remember."

"You didn't think that was odd?"

"Well, yeah at first—but he was such a nice guy, and he made it sound like I was doing him a big favor." She actually blushes like a little schoolgirl. She shrugs, "I didn't think that much about it."

As I sit there. I remember, clear as day, the look of anger on his face when I came home and told him I didn't remember rescheduling that appointment. I remember apologizing and feeling so terrible.

I sit at that table in the courtroom. There is a paper cup with water in front of me, and I drink it down. I've been up most of the night and so my head is a little fuzzy, but I try to concentrate as things move on. Jonny calls Mabel up there next, and I try to focus as he asks her about things. He even calls Boyd up there, although Boyd is mad and ornery, so I am not sure if that helps me or not. The judge starts telling Jonny that he needs to wrap this up—that he might use some of this in a trial but that he's not going to allow any more of it at this hearing. The judge calls both the lawyers up to talk to him.

And suddenly as I am sitting there, the edges of my vision start to go, and I feel that cold, clammy feeling like I'm about to pass out. I even open my mouth and turn my head to try to tell Jonny, but he just keeps on talking to the judge, while the room goes dark.

CHAPTER 40

Jean (2001)

When I come to, I am in the infirmary lying on a cot with a cool washcloth on my forehead. There is a nurse nearby, but her back is to me while she is flipping through a magazine, and I do not want to talk to anybody yet. I hope that hearing is just moving right along in my absence. I hope it is all over and done before I am well enough to go back.

It is still so hard for me to wrap my head around.

How could I have stayed? Why didn't I just leave? I suppose I'll ask myself that the rest of my life.

I think of his anger, or his exasperation when I would make some mistake or get something wrong. I think about that time he dropped me at the doctor's office downtown for a routine visit—my yearly. He was running some errands and was gonna come pick me up after. So I go do that exam that every woman hates, and come out of it feeling, as always, just a little bit violated. And I ride down the long elevator to the bottom and I get off and see Roger sitting there waiting in the main lobby of the building. He watches me as I step off the elevator and walk toward him. I can tell, already, by the way he holds his arms—a little stiff and set—that he is angry. In those few steps from the elevator over to him, my mind races, wondering if there was something I did that he could be angry about. Did I leave a load of clothes in the washer? A dish in the sink? Is there a mess on the kitchen counter? Was there something I was supposed to do but forgot? But he wasn't angry when he dropped me off, and he hasn't been home, he was at the hardware store. So it can't be about me. He must be angry at something else.

I smile as I walk up to him, hoping to make him feel better. His eyes are hard.

"Did you really think I wouldn't see that?"

"See what?" I ask.

"Have a nice elevator ride, did you?"

"What are you talking about Roger?"

"I saw you with that guy. I saw you smile at each other as you got off. Did you even go to the doctor? Did you even have an appointment? Or did you just meet up with him and go straight to the stairwell, or maybe the broom closet?"

"What the hell are you talking about?" My voice is loud— two women in the lobby turn to look at us. He has not raised his voice. To the outside world he sounds calm and rational, but to me he sounds like a lunatic. "Some guy was in the elevator when I got on—you sound crazy Roger!"

He stares at me, shakes he head as if he just can't believe me. Then, turns and walks back to the car. I stand there for a while, not really sure what to do. Then I go and get in the car. He is silent for a long time. Finally I say, "Roger, I don't understand what just happened. All I did was—"

"Why do you have to curse at me whenever we fight?" he asks. "Huh? Is it that difficult to respect me enough not to curse at me?"

"I didn't curse at you! I just said what the hell."

"You know I don't like cursing. Whenever we argue, you always end up there."

I am silent.

"Look, I am really hurt," he says. "I see you riding down on the elevator looking like you want to have this man's baby, and then when I say something to you, you start yelling and cursing at me."

"There just happened to be a guy on the elevator. I didn't even say 'Hello' to him."

"Well that's sure not what it looked like. And what? Am I supposed to just not say anything when you do something that makes me uncomfortable? I think I need to be able to say when I am feeling hurt by something without you lashing out and yelling and cursing."

"I wasn't yelling."

"You saw all those people looking at us—you were yelling."

I take a deep breath. Out of the corner of my eye, I see his hand on the car door handle. I know what he will do next. He will get out of the car, walk away and leave me there. And I will have to choose between driving away and leaving him or waiting for him to come back. I have no doubt.

I swallow. I push myself down, bury myself to keep the peace. "I'm sorry," I say.

He nods as if I should be, and his hand on the door handle relaxes a little,

Why didn't I get out then? Why didn't I just leave right then, before it got worse? I didn't know that I would just learn to live with it. I learned never to smile or joke with the clerk at the store or the Little League coach. Sometimes I would be outright rude to those people just so it was clear I was not being a flirt. I had no idea that eventually I would stop wearing lacy, pretty underwear, because I didn't want to deal with the questions—why I was wearing lacy underwear like that if there wasn't anyone special seeing me in it?

I learned to flatten myself, flatten my will, my desire. I learned to say only what was safe. *OK, sure honey. Of course, no problem. I don't know, whatever you think is fine.*" Those statements were my mantras. I was careful to laugh at his jokes. I was careful to laugh when he made fun of me because, of course, he was only joking, and if I took him seriously and asked him to stop, that would mean I was 'taking everything so seriously' and that I 'need to loosen up.' And if I were to say how it made me feel, all that sarcastic joking—how it was not funny over and over and over, especially when that was all there was—then he would go to the dark space where he would find something to be angry about for real. It was so much easier to just pretend to laugh.

Instead, as we drove home that day, I thought about the car. How if we'd just gotten my car fixed instead of selling it for scrap, I'd have been driving myself to the doctor's office and wouldn't have to deal with this. But when the transmission went, it was going to cost over three thousand dollars to fix it. Roger didn't think the old clunker was even worth that much and it seemed crazy to sink that kind of money into a car as old as mine was.

I wanted to look in the paper and find a good used car, but Roger had said, "Look, let's just save the money. I can drop you off at work before I go in."

"But what if you're out somewhere and I'm stuck at home? What if I just need to run an errand or something?"

"We'll work it out honey, that's what married people do. Besides, we need to save the money so we'll be ready to have that baby you want."

And my heart melted at that because it was true that I wanted a baby more than anything. And the small inconvenience of not being able to drive myself to the grocery store was nothing in comparison. So I gave in. I didn't think about the fact that the car we were giving up was my car, and the car we were keeping was his, which meant that if I ever wanted to go out to run and errand or something on a weekend when he was sitting around watching football, I would need to ask him if it was ok to take his car.

I hadn't realized that it meant if I wanted to meet some girlfriends for a movie, he'd offer to drive me and pick me up. He made it sound like he was doing me a favor. And the one time I told him it felt sort of funny and I'd rather just drive myself, he'd been hurt. Gotten all sulky and said, "I just thought it'd be nice for us to spend some time together, that's all. But if it's more important to you to be Miss Independent, that's fine, go on and have a good time."

All my looking forward to an evening with friends just sort of fizzled, like the air out of a balloon, and I knew if I drove myself, I would come home to the silent treatment until I apologized. So Roger dropped me off at the movie theater and was waiting for me when the movie got out. When all the other girls decided to go have a drink before heading home I told them sorry, maybe next time. Told them we were looking for a new car, but Roger had to drive me tonight. I made it sound light and airy, but inside it just felt sad.

Roger wasn't a yeller. He didn't call me bad names, never laid a hand on me. But it's like somehow he reached inside with invisible fingers and strangled everything that made me myself. I knew something was wrong. But he convinced me every time that it was me.

The next day after that fight about the elevator, I went outside and I saw Roger over in the neighbor's driveway, underneath the car like a mechanic. Mr. and Mrs. Ellis were standing out there, handing him a tool when he asked, and smiling when the engine started up just fine. Mr. Ellis smiled and clasped him on the back. And when I was close enough he said to me, "You're husband is a gift. Nicest guy in the world, this one. You are a lucky lady."

And I smiled and nodded. "Yes I am," I said.

And I could see it. He was the warm, funny, thoughtful man I married. And I put away that little part of me that wondered why he was not like that at home anymore. I put it far away and I told myself that marriage is about compromise, and I need to understand that being in a relationship means I don't have the same "freedom" I used to have. That's just part of being in a loving marriage—putting the other person first and making them a priority. If I could do that more, I thought, everything would be good at home.

And sometimes it was. Sometimes, for weeks, even months, we would get along, and we would laugh, and Roger was the kind, attentive man I married. And I told myself that those good patches were worth the bad patches. Once we had Lucas, I told myself he was a good father, and Lucas needed a good father. And mostly, I began to forget what it was like to be myself. To say what I really thought without knowing there would be a sarcastic, dismissive comment. To say what I really felt without fear it would be twisted into something very far from what I meant. So I worked to smooth myself out, until I was flat and still, like the smooth water on a quiet lake. I only reflected back to him what he wanted to see.

CHAPTER 41

Cora (1989)

Cora stood in the kitchen eating jalapenos straight from the jar, their spicy juice running down her fingers. She told herself she should stop—they would give her heartburn just before bed. But she felt such a compulsion—the pain of the spicy tang on her tongue just made her want more.

Suddenly, a sharp stab of pain doubled her over and she dropped the jar. She stared as it fell in slow motion. It hit the kitchen floor but didn't break, its juice spilling out all over the tiles. Her mind, numb with the pain, was confused for a moment, and she thought she must have spilled it down her front as it fell. But then she realized that the water that rushed out over her pajama bottoms and spread over the tiles to mingle with the jalapeno juice, came from her. Almost immediately, came another wave of pain, sharp and insistent.

Before she could call out, her mother was beside her, with a blanket to wrap Cora in, and an overnight bag.

"I told you it would be soon," her mother said, pointing at the full moon as they walked out the front door. "I've left a note for Bo. He can handle things here until we get back."

But Cora wondered. She didn't feel that it was because of the moon. She blamed the jalapenos. She had eaten as many of those tiny devilish fruits as her enormous stomach could hold over the last few months. And later, she wondered whether they were to blame for the baby's quirks—whether she had tainted forever the little life inside of her by her strange addiction.

For the moment the baby emerged, amidst the piercing screams and blinding pain, Cora knew she was different. Even before she had seen the baby, she saw the nurse turn her back and make the sign of the cross. And when Len was placed in Cora's arms, soft and sleeping, Cora marveled at her perfect little fingers and toes, and her shock of gray hair sticking straight out of her head like a troll doll. When Len opened her eyes and stared at her mother, it was with the wisest eyes Cora had ever seen. She was entranced with the beautiful, tiny creature in her arms.

The other nurse clucked her tongue and said "Don't worry, they all come out looking like little old folk—every one of 'em. It'll wear off and she'll be normal in no time, you'll see."

But Cora wasn't worried. She knew her baby was not normal. And why would she want normal anyway? She wanted this little bundle to stay just as she was, always, with her wise eyes able to see everything inside of her.

When Cora woke, the sheets were cool on her skin, and she reached immediately for the plastic cup of water on the tray beside her bed, funneling the straw into her mouth as if she were an old lady. There was an electricity in her body—a euphoria that made her wide awake despite her exhaustion. Her mother was not in the room, but her presence was marked by the bag stuffed with a newspaper and the half cup of coffee on the low table.

The room was quiet except for the electric buzzing noise that never went away. She dragged herself out of bed, the floor cold on her feet, and walked a few steps to the crib. Len lay wrapped, snuggly like a little pea pod, her eyes closed and her tuft of thick hair sticking up almost straight. She lifted her, smelled her soft, fuzzy head as she kissed it. The joy she felt was marred only by the image in her mind of Edison beside her—the way she wanted it to be deep in her heart. But she shook the image away and held the baby tight.

CHAPTER 42

Cora (1990)

For the first year, Cora tried to keep up with her classes, determined to do all the reading as if she were still in school. She knew she had it easy being able to stay at home, her mother still running the ranch so there wasn't much for her to do to help out anyway. She'd get her reading done while Len napped, sometimes while she was playing quietly in her crib. Cora made diligent notes, still thinking that one day she would go back to school, and when she did she would need to be ready to finish her thesis. But at some point along the way, it became impossible to do any work during the hours Len was awake. She was an active baby, and when she began to crawl, and then walk, Cora couldn't have her attention on anything else. If she wanted to really get any work done, she realized finally, she would need to hire a babysitter.

Sometimes Cora would leave the baby with her ma and do something. Usually what she chose to do was take a nap, or a bubble bath, or read a book. But it wasn't often—not because her mother didn't offer, but because Cora didn't want to miss a moment. When Len smiled, the whole world made sense to Cora. She saw things so differently now. And when she rocked the baby to sleep playing Modern English, the songs took on an entirely different meaning. Len would snuggle like a little monkey, fitting perfectly into Cora's shoulder. There was no greater feeling of peace.

Cora knew Len was special. She noticed that often, after the baby's bath, the water swirled clockwise as it drained. She saw the way the birds would come, just to sit beside the baby when she strapped her into the little bouncy chair and brought it outside while she gardened. People who were broken and damaged in some way were drawn to Len like a magnet. Cora would take her into town, pushing her in the stroller, and every sad, lonely, injured person they encountered would want to see her.

Everyone loves a baby, Cora knew that—everyone coo'd and smiled at how cute she was, that was a given. But there was a difference. The way Old Man Tate came over and asked quietly, reverently if he could touch the baby—his eyes clear and intelligent, as if he didn't spend all his time on the street corner yelling epithets to passersby. The way Maggie Reynolds, limping with her hip out of whack, looked crazed, almost possessed as she neared them and reached out gently to stroke Len's foot. This all made Cora careful when she brought the baby into town. But eventually she realized that there was only so much she would be able to shield Len from. For even in her dreams, Len was special.

It was after midnight when Cora woke one night, feeling pulled to Len's nursery without knowing why. Cora placed her bare feet on the floorboards and walked quietly into the hall. The door to the nursery was halfway open, as she'd left it, and she saw the glow of the night light, just as it should be. She almost turned and went right back to bed. But then she heard Len laugh. Len was a year old by then, still in the early stages of walking, and her laugh was something that could light the entire house with joy. She laughed when Walter picked her up and swung her gently in circles until she got dizzy. She laughed when the dog put his slobbery face next to hers and let him pull on his ears. And she would laugh when Cora blew raspberries on her plump little tummy. This laugh was no different. There was nothing alarming about it, except that it was the middle of the night and Len should have been sleeping instead of awake and laughing.

Cora leaned in, pushing the door the rest of the way open. But there was Len, curled comfortably in her crib, her breathing steady. Cora glanced around the room, and there was nothing amiss. In her sleep, Len's little mouth turned up in a smile, and she giggled. Cora smiled watching her and turned to go. But suddenly she froze. There was a flicker of movement by the crib, and when she looked more closely, she saw it. A long snake, entwined around the corner bedpost.

Cora gasped and reached out to quickly to pluck Len out of the crib. Len woke, groggy and unsure, but as soon as she opened her eyes she turned her head to look directly at the snake, who was slithering down the bedpost. She lifted her hand and made the waving motion she'd just learned along with the word, opening and closing the fingers of her fist. "Bye bye," she whispered as the snake slithered out the door. Cora followed the snake, trying to figure out how to catch or kill the thing—the last thing she wanted was a loose snake in the house. But it made its way quickly out to the living room, and straight out the window that had been left open to the evening air. Cora plopped Len onto the sofa as she shut the window forcefully and turned the lock. By the time Cora turned to pick up Len again, she was sound asleep.

CHAPTER 43

Jean (2001)

Before we head into the hearing the next day, Jonny tells me that Roger is out of his coma. The doctors say he is recovering well, and they think he'll be going home at the end of the week. He'll have to use a cane, and he'll probably never lose the limp, but he'll be able to go home. I don't know why the hell he's gonna have a limp when I shot him in the chest, but I don't ask. I reckon I should be happy. I reckon I should be relieved I haven't committed a murder and that Lucas's father is still alive.

But the honest truth is, I am more than slightly disappointed. I never want to see Roger again. I never want to speak to him again. I do not want him interfering in my life and taking Lucas away from me. Truth is, when I thought he was going to die, I felt free. But I know he's not gonna leave me alone. I know he will try to warp and twist things and try to get me under his thumb again.

I try not to think about all that as I walk into the courtroom. I am led straight to the witness stand and I swear to God to tell the truth. When I start talking, it is like everything I have been thinking about in here just comes out of my mouth. Jonny asks me questions, and the other lawyer asks me questions, but mostly I just talk. I tell that judge all about those things Roger did to me. I tell about how I used to be, before we were married, before I even met Roger. And I tell him what my married life was like and how confused I was and how I thought for sure I was crazy.

When I really think about it, I figure there must have been some part of me that was acting in self-defense when I shot him. I mean, he wasn't trying to kill me—not my body anyways. But what he did was kill the inside of me. He did it so slow I did not even notice until I looked around after that shot rang out, and in the stillness and the silence, I did not know who I was anymore. I think I shot him that night because I realized it was either him or me.

When they are all done asking me questions, Jonny takes my elbow and helps me back to my seat. His face is drawn and his lips are tight, and I think that probably means I didn't do so good. I know that what I did doesn't count as self-defense no matter how you look at it. I know I am probably gonna be stuck here for fifteen years like Jonny told me I might. But I already knew that coming into this hearing this morning, and there wasn't nothing I could say to change that. And since I told that judge my story, I feel better than I have in a long time.

Jonny stands in the corner talking to the District Attorney. After a while he comes back to the table and says, "Jean, the judge is deliberating, probably won't have a decision for a couple of hours. I've just been speaking with the D.A. He wants to offer you a plea bargain."

I look up at him, not sure if this is a good thing or not. He smiles. "It's a good deal, Jean. They are offering if you plead guilty to second degree aggravated assault, they'll let you do six months jail time and two years community supervision."

I stare at him.

"Jean, you were looking at a probably fifteen years, possibly even longer. This is an incredibly good deal for you. All that stuff you said up on the witness stand today, that helps a lot to explain why you did what you did. It helps other people make sense of it. But it wouldn't get you off the hook if the judge comes back in a couple of hours with a decision that they can go ahead and try you for first degree attempted murder. They know that too." He nods at the D.A. "They just also know that Roger and his family don't want this big trial. It turns out they've decided they want this all to be over just as much as we do, so the D.A. promised them he'd try to strike a deal."

He is waiting, waiting for me to laugh, smile, jump up and down, I don't know what. I don't feel happy though, I just feel tired. Because here is the other fucked up thing: if Roger is alive, then it actually seems pretty alright to be here in prison away from him. But I don't say that. I think about my mama, and about Lucas, and I say, "OK Jonny. That sounds like a pretty good deal to me."

CHAPTER 44
Cora (2001)

It's been a long time since Cora has wanted to take anything stronger than a Sudafed. Taking a pill to alter your mood is something she associates with another lifetime, something she'd done just for fun. The goal had always been to expand her experience; it was never because she felt like she needed to take something to get by. Never before because she was a nervy mess, and if she didn't have some sort of help calming her nerves she would self-destruct and would never even make it to late afternoon when they plan to head to the venue. It is still morning. She sips her coffee instead.

She wonders if Edison is staying in a hotel somewhere, or if he's just sleeping in the tour bus. She and Len could go anytime, this was their sole purpose for being here. It's not as though there is anything else to occupy their time. But Cora knows that once they are there, knocking on the door of an empty bus or sitting in their car in an empty parking lot, each minute will seem an hour.

Cora wracks her brain yet again for some other way she could go about this. It seems completely ridiculous that in this day and age, when all you have to do is type someone's name into the computer and you can learn anyone's life story, that it should come to this. But here was the thing—you had to type a full name—and it always came back to that silly little thing. She hadn't even known his last name. They'd met in a club for God's sake. Who asks someone for a last name in a club? Yes, of course at some point it would come up wouldn't it? It just never had. And she had never thought of it. It had never occurred to her to ask. She had thought she had all the time in the world.

Cora walks out to the pool with a broad brimmed hat to shield her face from the sun, and lays out on a lounge chair at the far end of the pool, far enough away from the girls that she's not infringing on their space. She forces herself to wait. Forces herself to take the girls to the diner across the street for lunch, to lie down and try to nap afterward, and finally, about midafternoon, she decides she's made herself wait long enough. She walks out to the pool, over to where Len is stretched out in the shade of an umbrella reading.

"What do you think, honey? You ready to head over there soon?"

Len looks at her with a serious face and nods. Against her better judgment, Cora had promised Rachel and Doris they could come too. 'In case you or Len need anything' was how Doris put it.

The parking lot is empty. At least it looks that way when Cora first pulls in. The tour bus is nowhere in sight and Cora's heart sinks. She circles the building and parks near the back entrance—it is propped open but she can't see any lights inside. They slowly get out of the car, and Cora takes a deep breath, and leads the way.

CHAPTER 45
Len (2001)

This is it. There is no turning back now. The day of reckoning. The day I will finally meet my daddy. It's funny, so often I get a feeling about how something is going to go—a big test at school, a holiday, or whatever—but this time I don't. I have absolutely no idea how this is going to go down.

The concert hall is not one of those massive sports stadiums. It is called a "music center" and basically it is just a smaller, cleaner, nicer version of a stadium, with a fancy sign out front. I get out of the car and the heat from the blacktop hits my legs in waves. There is a sizzle in the air—it makes it a little hard to breathe.

"We'll just wait out here in the shade while ya'll go ahead in," Mrs. Corbin says.

Ma grabs my hand like I'm a little kid, but I let her lead me towards the back of the building where there's an entrance to the backstage area.

There is no security guard or anything, so we just march right in. Guys in black T-shirts are milling around, setting up equipment. One of them comes over to us.

"Sorry guys, you're not allowed to be in here."

Ma looks right at him and says, "I need to talk to Edison."

The guy shakes his head. "I don't know any Edison."

She laughs. "Sorry, I mean Clifton, his real name is Edison. It's very important."

He cocks his head like he's heard that before. "Look, you can't be back here, lady. But he's not here anyway."

I can tell Ma is about to pitch a fit, but just then a guy with a massive chest sporting the word 'security' comes over and inserts himself between them.

"Scotty, close the door next time," he calls over his shoulder as he escorts us back out the way we came in.

Mrs. Corbin is standing outside, and she raises her eyebrows in a question as we emerge into the sunlight. Ma shakes her head and Mrs. Corbin looks disappointed. We stand there for a while, not sure what to do.

"Well, he'll have to get here sooner or later," Ma says. "And this is the only entrance I can see except for the front. He may be famous, but he still has to walk through an entrance eventually."

It is hot, and I can feel the waves of heat coming up from the asphalt.

"We're just supposed to sit here and wait?" I ask. "This is really not a very well thought-out plan, is it Cora?"

"Don't call me Cora," she says, but her heart isn't in it.

She looks a little lost. I take her hand. "It's okay," I tell her. "We're going to see him today."

Just then Rachel comes around the corner of the building. She has twisted her shirt up and tied it so that her midriff shows above her cutoffs. She walks right up to us, and I can't figure out the grin on her face until she pulls her hand out from behind her back to reveal two backstage passes clipped onto lanyards. Every one of our mouths drops open at the sight.

"No!" Ma exclaims in disbelief.

"What?!" I cry. "No way!"

"Way," she nods, her eyes twinkling, clearly proud of herself. "The dude up in the front was a little lonely. Just wanted to chat for a while."

"Oh my God, I don't believe it. Thank you!" Ma cries. Then she narrows her eyes at Rachel and says, "Honey, did you have to do anything other than talk to him to get these?"

Rachel rolls her eyes. "God no—he wasn't even cute!" She smiles, and it is clear how that smile alone could convince someone of almost anything. I don't doubt her even for a second, and I give her a big hug as she hands me a lanyard.

We pass the time at the diner across the street, and Ma keeps an eagle eye on the parking lot. When she sees the tour bus pull in, she stands up. Mrs. Corbin gives Ma a big hug and pats my hand. They will take a taxi back to the hotel so we can take whatever time we need. Ma looks at me. We are asking each other, silently, if we are ready.

CHAPTER 46

Cora (2001)

I t seems like the longest hallway Cora's ever seen in her life. It stretches from the door at the back of the stadium to a large room at the end where there is a crowd already gathered. Cora flashes her pass to the bouncer and Len does the same. Together they walk with purpose toward the crowd at the end of the hall. Cora's stomach is doing flips, and she feels a bit faint. Maybe she should have worn a skirt instead of jeans—she'd been trying for the 'not trying too hard' look. She'd worked hard on her makeup so that it looked like she wasn't wearing any. She'd wanted to look cool, not so much like a mom. But it really couldn't be helped, and anyway it made absolutely no difference now. She was not here for herself, she was here for Len.

But still, Cora's steps slow as they near the end of the hallway, and before they reach it, she stops completely. There is a moment when she is not sure she can go on. It has been the thing she has lived with for so many years now, the humiliation and pain. In many ways it was so long ago. But to her, as always, it feels like just yesterday.

There is another large bouncer at the end of the hallway, and Cora makes sure her pass is visible. There's a small crowd, and when she and Len walk up, a lady with a clipboard appears. She is lovely. She does not look like a mom. She looks like she wakes up fresh faced and smelling of lavender. Cora's heart sinks.

"Okay, where are my contest winners?" the woman asks, checking the list on her clipboard. A small group departs into the next room, and the rest stay behind. This is not the way things had been in the venues she had gotten backstage in when she was younger. Cora remembered loud music and smoke and band members joking and laughing surrounded by swooning groupies desperate for attention. Cora was expecting a party. This is more like waiting for a doctor's appointment.

Cora nudges her way forward so she can see inside the room a little. "Don't worry lady, you'll get your turn," the bouncer says.

Cora gives him a side eye. "Why can't we just go inside? What's with the waiting in line thing?"

Len rolls her eyes. "Ma," she says in a 'please stop embarrassing me' tone.

Cora sighs. "Whatever."

But as soon as the lady with the clipboard returns, Cora says, "Yeah, I'm not sure what all this waiting in line thing is about, but I just need to get in to talk to Edison."

The lady looks surprised at the use of his name. "Don't worry Ma'am, you'll get your turn."

Ma'am? So that was how it was going to be?

"Well, it's just that I brought his daughter to see him." She puts her arm around Len as she speaks.

Ms. Clipboard turns to the bouncer, who stands up a little straighter.

"I'm not a crazed fan. I promise. Can you please just tell him that Cora Walker is here and he has a daughter he's never met."

The bouncer steps forward. "Look lady, I need you to calm down or we'll have to ask you to leave."

Len reaches out and takes Cora's hand, and a feeling of calm spreads through Cora's arm all through her body.

"It's okay," Len says sweetly to the clipboard. "My mom's just excited—she hasn't seen my dad in like, a really long time. Don't worry, we'll just wait 'til everyone else has gone in first." She tugs on Cora, who stays quiet as the clipboard lady gives them both a sharp look and ushers the next group of teenagers wearing cowboy boots and lip gloss down the hallway.

The wait seems to last forever, and finally it is just the two of them, Len and Cora, staring at their feet while they wait for the clipboard to return. Finally, she does, her face serious. There are no more fake polite smiles full of sparkling white teeth.

"I'm sorry, Ma'am." She does not look sorry as she speaks. "Mr. Wilkes says you have the wrong guy. He doesn't know anyone named Cora."

Cora had prepared herself for this moment ever since she had glimpsed Edison's face on the TV screen in Roger's hospital room. But she worries now, that she has completely neglected to prepare Len for this possibility. She glances over at her daughter, but Len is not crushed, she is staring hard at the woman. Then she actually laughs.

"Yes he does," Len exclaims. "It's all over your face that he does." But then she is quiet, the implication suddenly dawning on her, that if he knows, his failure to appear means that he doesn't want to see her.

Before Cora can react, all of a sudden, there he is, standing in the back room so that they can see him through the doorway. No one says anything for a long time.

Cora feels like the wind has been knocked out of her. It is a good thing she saw a picture of him first—she's not surprised at how his face had filled out and how there are small wrinkles at the corners of his eyes. She wonders if he is experiencing a wave of shock as he looks at her; whether he has to search to see in her the person that he had known so long ago. But then she remembers that of course it wouldn't be as much of a shock for him. She was just a fling he had a long time ago. It would be different for him. When her eyes meet his, the rest of the world falls away for a moment. There is sadness there, a flicker of anger that she doesn't understand, but mostly sadness. No one says a word.

It is only when his eyes leave hers and he looks at Len that she can breathe again. She pulls Len over in front of her, hands on her shoulders. It is a long time before he looks back at Cora.

"What are you doing here, Cora?" His voice is calm, the sadness in his eyes still there.

She had planned this so carefully. She had mapped out her route, her strategy, and how she would get here and be able to meet him. How had she not planned out exactly what she would say to him? Nothing seems quite right.

"I need to tell you about Len," she says. "She's your daughter." That is not what she meant to say—she didn't mean to just blurt it out like that. She mentally kicks herself as they stand again in an awkward silence.

He looks again at Len, then turns away and shakes his head. "You always wanted to be on your own. I reckon you'll keep on doing just fine without me."

"No—we're not fine—Len's not fine. She doesn't know her father. She deserves to know you."

"After all this time—all these years…? Why'd you come here like this? Why like this?" he shakes his head and turns away. "Do you need money or something? Is that what it is? And her real father is what? MIA and can't help you out so you thought you'd cash in on me now that the pockets are jingling a little—is that it?"

The anger that had been a glimmer behind his eyes is out in the open now, clear in the sneer of his words as he speaks. Before Cora can say anything at all, he simply walks away. "I can't help you Cora," he says as he leaves.

Cora needs to be strong. She needs to be there for Len. She thinks of this as she makes the long walk back down the hallway to the outside door. She holds Len's hand tightly, as if she were a small child again. But by the time they walk outside into the moon bright night, Cora is sucking air and almost doubled over.

It is the absolute certainty that crushes her. All these years she has lived without knowing. She has lived with the possibility, so very small and distant, but the possibility nonetheless, that one day she could have him back. The possibility that he really had loved her despite the way things turned out. And the crush of that possibility now flattens her.

She had thought of this expedition as being about Len. It was something she needed to do for her daughter. That thought had given her strength and purpose. It had given her the courage to do what she would never otherwise have done.

But she realizes now she has not prepared either of them for this scenario.

She sits on the curb by the parking lot, stunned and trying to breathe. Len sits beside her and puts an arm around her. "It's okay Ma."

Cora shakes her head. "It's not okay. I should never have brought you here. What was I thinking? I can't believe I thought this would ever be alright. I can't believe I just let you see firsthand what an asshole your father is!"

Len nods. "That was pretty asshole behavior," she agrees.

"Yeah, that's the understatement of the year."

"I don't think he really meant all that though."

"If he didn't mean it, why would he say it? And it doesn't really matter anyway, I mean a rejection is a rejection—it doesn't really matter much why, does it?"

"I think it sort of does matter though."

Cora realizes she needs to try to be the parent here. "You know, honey—that was not a rejection of you. It was most definitely a rejection of me." She thinks for a moment. "Well, I guess it just justifies my raising you all on my own though doesn't it?"

"Well, it's not like you had a choice in that matter, did you Ma?" But when Len sees how crushed Cora is she says, "Sorry, I didn't mean it like that."

"No, you're right," Cora says. "He's a jerk. We don't need him though do we, honey? Me and you against the world, just like always, right?"

"Sure Ma." Len pats her on the back.

CHAPTER 47

Len (2001)

I have been waiting my whole life for the moment I would meet my daddy. But the moment I actually see him, flesh and blood and right in front of me, it is not how I imagined.

I am holding Ma's hand, and I feel her pulse quicken and her blood go cold. And suddenly, down the long hallway and in the full light of the open room in front of us, there he is. I don't feel a lightning bolt of love and connection like I thought I would. I don't feel a swoosh of completeness, like the missing piece in the puzzle of my life has finally fallen into place. But I don't feel a searing pang of emptiness and rejection either. At least, not at first.

It is sort of like the rest of the world goes a bit fuzzy—the only thing that is in focus is the man in the room. He is tall and fit, and I am not just saying this because he is my daddy, but he is very, very handsome, even with his jaw set hard and a bit of a scowl on his face. He does not look at me. It is like he is trying his hardest, with all his might, not to look at me. There is absolutely no chance that he will rush over to me with tears in his eyes because of his happiness that I exist.

He is saying something. His voice, and Ma's voice back and forth are like noises through the water. I know they are talking, but I can't make out the words. I focus my hardest, and the sound begins to clear.

"What is it? You need money?" he is asking Ma. "Is that why you got in touch after all these years?

They are speaking in strained voices, and the whole time, despite the words that talk about how they are not connected,

I can see it, clear as day. There are little strings of lightning that stretch all the way along the hallway, reaching from her to him. They bounce and vibrate a little with the words, but I can see them, bright and happy.

But in spite of the lightning, he turns us away, after barely even looking at me. Ma is deflated, beaten down with it all. And I just feel empty. I know he is lying when he says he doesn't want to see her. And I know he is lying when he says he doesn't believe he is my daddy. In a way, that's what makes it all worse.

CHAPTER 48

Jean (2001)

I wait for Bonnie-Lynn in the library for almost an hour. I listen to the low murmur from a couple of girls in the back, and the rustle of paper as someone thumbs through a book. I like the quiet—the stale, musty smell. This is the last time I will see Bonnie-Lynn. They're gonna let me out soon, and to be perfectly honest, I have mixed feelings about that. Because as messed up as it sounds, I have had my first taste of freedom in years in this here facility. There are bars around me most of the time, and I am told where to go and what to do. But other than those things, they basically leave us alone. No one is messing with my mind here. I am learning to trust what I say to other people. Being alone is what most people hate about this place, but the God's honest truth is that I have enjoyed that part immensely.

So I am not counting the hours until I get out of here. As I wait for Bonnie-Lynn I thumb through the pages of one of the big law books stacked on the table. That time when I was under Roger's thumb seems far away from me now. So far away that it is hard for me to think about how it all started. I think about that time, not long after we got married, when Roger got so angry because I hadn't mixed the salad dressing together enough—the oil and vinegar not shaken up enough, so they separated on the leaves. I remember my surprise at his reaction. I mean, it was just salad dressing, and his anger seemed to come out of nowhere. He'd said that if I cared about him, I would pay attention to things I knew he cared about. I laugh a little now, remembering it—even though I know it is not funny. I know that when I let that sort of thing go, I was letting myself go. I could have put my foot down in the beginning—but it seemed awfully silly to be arguing about salad dressing. And then it was because I didn't fold the laundry the right way, and when I didn't let him know I was planning to run some errands after work—where was the line when it became too much?

How was I to know where that was all leading? I had no way of knowing how bad it would get. I was used to being independent. I was used to a family that let me make my own decisions. It never occurred to me to expect anything else.

The one thing I do miss in here is Lucas. I think about hugging him long and hard when I get out, even though he will roll his eyes and I'll try not to cry. I will ruffle his hair and let him play video games as long as he wants. There are other things I am looking forward to when I get out, that's for damn sure. I am looking forward to a soft comfortable bed and a hot shower I can stay in for as long as I want. I am already thinking of going to the grocery store and picking out a big thick steak and some bright green asparagus. I am thinking I can go home and cook the steak to soft pink in the middle and the asparagus to crisp and crunchy, and I can slather both with butter and sit anywhere I damn please to eat it all.

I sit there thinking of all those things until it is almost time to go back to my cell. Lizzy, the lady who has the much-envied job of helping to run the library most days, comes over. She's older, which makes her stand out a bit. She seems more like one of the ladies that would be working in the cafeteria at Lucas's middle school or something, her stringy brown hair caught up in a hair net. But here she is quiet and respected, left alone most of the time.

"You're not waiting on Bonnie-Lynn are you?" she asks.

"Yeah," I say. "I sure am.

"She ain't coming," Lizzy says.

"Why not?"

"She got solitary. Can't believe you didn't hear."

I shake my head. "What for?"

"Fight in the yard. They say she sliced up the other girl so bad she had to go to the hospital. And I mean the real hospital, not this school nurse's office they got here."

"Sliced her?" I ask, "You mean with a knife?"

She rolls her eyes and looks at me like I'm an idiot. "Yeah, a knife. Whadya think?" She turns and walks away from me shaking her head and laughing to herself, "With a knife? Oh Lordy."

I should not be surprised. This place is a shithole, I am aware of that fact. And the people in here are all sorts of messed up. But I never saw that side of Bonnie-Lynn. I remind myself, as I make my way back to my cell, that I need to be vigilant. I need to be always on my guard. I will get out soon. I just need to keep my head down until then.

It seems that the other girls do not get the memo about me keeping things quiet until I get out. Or maybe they know exactly what I am trying to do but don't give a rat's ass. The girl in the hospital is named Bacon. At least that's what they all call her. And I have learned that her friends are not happy about her predicament. Bonnie-Lynn has other friends in here, I am not the only one. But I am certainly the weakest one. They know an easy target when they see one.

I keep my guard up as I walk through the lunch line. I have learned a thing or two. The utensils are plastic, but clearly Bonnie-Lynn was able to get her hands on something a little stronger than that, so I know it is possible. There are whispers, looks that mean things. It is a foreign language that I have only learned a little bit of during my time here. I can only hope I know enough.

I eat my lunch slowly, sitting at the end of the table. I am not alone, but I am not next to anyone of significance. I make myself eat, because I recognize there may come a moment where I will need my strength.

It doesn't happen until we are out in the yard. There are guards that are supposed to watch what happens out here. Most of the time they do, but they are as bored as we are mainly, so it is no surprise really that they are not constantly vigilant. I keep to myself, walk the worn path along the edge of the yard to get a little exercise. But I stay where the guards can see me the whole time.

I am in broad sight when the three girls start walking with me. They don't say anything, just fall into step with me, so close I can hear their breathing. I know what they are thinking. I know what they are planning to do. But I am not cut out for this. Maybe if I'd been here long enough to learn a few more things. Maybe if I'd gotten harder, listened better and paid more attention. But as it is, I know just enough to know that I am in deep trouble, but not enough to get myself out of it. I'm just a mom—I was in the PTA, for Christ's sake.

When it happens, I learn that I am good at one thing. I can scream loud and long, so that everyone almost anywhere can hear me. It is not exactly what I'd hoped for. I wish that I were also good at one other thing—that would be running. Because I scream loud and hard, and I start running. But although my yell is enough to curdle yogurt in the fridge, my running does not get me too far and when they are all on top of me I feel a hot searing pain across my arm. I am thrashing and yelling so much that when things shift and change and strong hands reach in to help me up, I am still thrashing so much that someone has to slap me across the face to get me to stop.

They take me to the infirmary and stich me up. It's not really too bad—five stiches is all. And because I am shaking and terrified of going back out there, and on top of that I'm getting out so soon it hardly matters anymore, the Warden lets me stay in the separate unit I didn't even know they had. I don't know who usually gets to stay there—maybe fancy prisoners like famous people or politicians or something. But the bed is a little softer, and the meals are a little warmer, and I don't have to see anybody else. And this, I can handle. This is a piece of cake.

CHAPTER 49

Jean (2001)

They let me out on a Tuesday. Ma is waiting for me. She even brings me a little bag with some powder and lipstick and a change of clothes. I hug her for a very long time. And when I let go, there are tears in both our eyes. She nods and pats my hand. She brushes my hair for me in the bathroom, and we head out the door into the bright sunlight.

I have been outside during the past weeks, but the air in the courtyard didn't feel like this, and the sun in the courtyard didn't feel like this. I turn my face up to the sun and breathe for just a moment.

Ma drives. Her hands are tight on the wheel and she talks through thin lips. About how she has a bed made up for me, and how Roger's ma already agreed to let Lucas come over once a week. She looks down, a little embarrassed, when she explains that one of the conditions is that she has to be there with me the whole time. "They didn't even have to agree," Ma says, trying to make it sound like something not so terrible. "The lawyer wanted them to stick with the two-hour supervised visitation that the Court ordered."

I nod as I listen. I let her handle it all for now. I have been a little preoccupied.

"When's he coming?" I ask.

"Tomorrow."

I am not sure how to feel. It is a remarkable thing to feel nervous about seeing your own son. I remember the time I spent walking on eggshells in my own home. Not laughing with Lucas like I wanted to because Roger was busy watching a show, not letting Lucas eat popcorn upstairs while he watched a movie because Roger would be mad at him if he spilled. Those were the little things. Would he ever know the big ones? All the times I told Roger I had done something so that Lucas wouldn't get yelled at? The time we were out to dinner and Roger got mad about something and just left us there? He'd ordered dinner and everything, then just left us. I don't even remember what he got mad about. Lucas was about eight. Plenty old enough to wonder where Dad went and why he left us. Would he ever know how much it took for me to laugh and smile and say lightly, "Daddy's so silly, he forgot he had to be at work." And when we took the bus home afterward, how hard it was for me to keep the tears in until we got home and he was tucked in bed. Why didn't I call a ride? Why didn't I call Ma? But I don't have to think about it but a minute, I know why I didn't. Because if I told her, if I'd told anyone, it would have made it real. I wouldn't have been able to go back to pretending things were fine after that. And by then I did not have the energy to leave.

Ma drives as she always does, steady and slow. We turn down our street, toward the house I grew up in. The sunlight drifts, mottled, through the trees lining the road. I picture me and Cisley running through the dry leaves in the fall, kicking a ball around with the other kids on the block. I remember, for a moment, what it felt like. To be the older one. To be the one in charge when our parents left the house. The one who got good grades and was responsible. Those were things I was good at. I remember that feeling.

I have to think for a long time to remember the last time I visited my mama. It was a very long time ago. Entirely too long.

Ma acts as if I am a child. She takes my bag, sits me on the sofa and makes tea. The house is the same. The same worn furniture, covered with doilies in an attempt to look fresh. The same smell even—fresh bread and pine—the smell of my youth. I remember doing puzzles on the coffee table where my tea sits, steaming. That was another thing I was good at, puzzles.

"Thanks Ma," I say as she sits beside me.

She reaches over and takes my hand, holds it in hers. We sit for a while like that, just listening to the birds outside.

That night, I sleep in my old childhood room. It was made into Ma's sewing room years ago, but it was never painted over, and the old twin sized bed is still there for guests. For a long time, I sit on that bed, remembering who I was. I nestle down between the sheets, and I remember. I remember being the girl who got scabby knees from learning how to ride a bike. The girl who's feet turned calloused and hard every summer from running barefoot. The girl who whispered with Cisley until we laughed so hard we almost peed our pants.

That girl has been gone for a long time, but I remember her now. I remember what it felt like to be her—what my body felt like, free and confident, the way it felt to laugh and joke without worrying how someone else would react. I curl up, soft and warm in the blankets that smell like home. I know I will wake up and take a cup of coffee out to the back porch and listen to the sparrows and the killdeer. And I will turn my face up to the warming sun, and I will be able to breathe in freedom.

CHAPTER 50
Cora (2001)

Cora is quiet as they drive back to the hotel. She feels broken, numb. For years after Edison left and as Len grew, she had wished for closure. Sometimes she even had the morbid thought that if they'd stayed together and he had died, it would have been better, because at least she would have had closure. She would have been able to mourn him and then move on with her life.

She'd never been able to have it out with him, tell him what a jerk he was. She'd been cheated of that moment and for so long it had felt unfair. And now she is kicking herself. She finally had the opportunity, and she'd completely failed. But, she reminds herself, this trip was not for her, this confrontation was not about her. Still, she replays the entire scene, over and over as she drives. And she tries not to think about how good he still looked, how his brown eyes and tousled hair still disarmed her, and how her legs turned to jelly when he looked at her.

She pulls into the parking lot of the motel only mildly curious about the police car with lights flashing parked in front, until she sees the officer, notebook open, talking to Doris.

"What on earth?" Cora whispers. Doris looks distraught, moving her arms back and forth as she talks.

Cora gets out of the car and walks over, touching Doris on the shoulder gently.

"It's Rachel," Doris says, turning towards her. "She went with her father."

The officer is sympathetic, jotting down notes about the make and model of the truck.

"I'll need to see a copy of the restraining order also, Ma'am."

Doris freezes for a moment. "I…I don't know if I brought it with me—I never expected to see him out here."

"Well, does he have any visitation rights at all?"

"Yes, but we are supposed to meet at a public place at a certain time—he's not supposed to come near my home."

The officer nods. "I see." He looks down at his notebook. "You see, it's just that, this is a public place. You're staying here, but it's not your home. That's why I sorta need to see the actual restraining order to see what it says about that sort of situation."

"I don't have it with me. I know right where it is in my desk at home. I just didn't ever think to bring it with me."

"Well, here's what I think you need to do then." The officer closes his notebook and clicks his pen closed. "You go on back home, get your court order, and talk to your attorney. There ain't really a whole lot we can usually do for you anyhow, since the restraining order, like you said, doesn't say he can't come near your daughter. It's just about you and your home."

Doris nods. Cora can see she is fighting back tears. The policeman slowly puts his notebook in his shirt pocket, nods to them and heads back to his car.

"How did he know where you were?" Cora asks Doris.

"I think she must have called him." She pulls a tissue from her pocket and blows her nose hard. "Rachel must have called him."

"Did she ask him to come get her?"

"I don't know. I don't know why she would do that. She knows what he is like—she knows."

CHAPTER 51

Len (2001)

I wake in the middle of the night. I can hear Ma's steady breathing in the other bed. But there is no soft snoring from Rachel's mom, and I don't see her bulky form under the blankets. The red numbers on the clock say 2:11. I try to go back to sleep, but I keep picturing my father, avoiding looking me in the eye. And I keep picturing his back walking away. I am empty, hollowed out.

There is something inside of me that feels broken. I thought for so long that finding my daddy would fix it. I had been certain that it would. But when I was daydreaming about that event, it always seemed to turn out a little differently. It did not end up in my dream that I'd find myself stuck with probably two of the loneliest women on the planet, in a cheap motel room that smells like feet, with my daddy just around the corner ignoring us all and being adored by a stadium full of fans. That was never the ending I envisioned.

Suddenly, I need to be outside. The indoor air is stuffy, and I need to feel the earth. I need to breath in the wind and hear what it says to me. I need to know what is in store. I slip quietly out of bed, and out the door into the warm night. Everything around me is cold and concrete. There is no earth for me to sink my feet into, no grass to carry the melody in the wind. And so I move instead to the water. It is mutated, antiseptic, chlorinated water, but at least it is water.

I sit at the edge of the pool and roll up my pajama bottoms over my knees. I dangle my feet in the water. It is warm, soothing. I sit and I think about my daddy. My whole life there has been a raw space inside of me. My whole life I have thought that if I could just find him, that space would be filled up. But I never thought it would just be knowing who he was that would fill it—I always imagined it where my father became a part of my life. Where he would teach me to shoot straight and how to fix the tractor. Where he would tell me I was beautiful and call me his princess. Where he would drop me at school and call out, "Bye Honey, love you," like the other dads. Where he would kiss me goodnight and be there again when I woke up in the morning. I don't quite know what to make of this turn of events.

I hear a hum in the background as I move my feet gently in the water. I close my eyes and the hum moves all along inside me, little ripples as I move my feet. When I open my eyes, the water is brighter, illuminated by something I can't see. I slip gently down into the pool, sinking all the way under. At first, feelings hit me in waves—excitement, like a child feeling the thrill of new places, love, the parent for the child, sadness, someone visiting an ailing relative—and I think I must be feeling the waves of all the people who have swum in this water. I am feeling every emotion you can even name, all just passing through me in little ripples.

But then I open my eyes under water and the light is all around me. The feelings stop coming, and the light is warm and comforting. I think for a moment how easy it would be to just stay here, listening to this hum forever. But then in a flash, I see my Ma's face, and I burst up into the air again, gasping for breath. The image was so vivid I expect to see her standing there, but there is no one. Just me, dripping wet in the moonlight. I grab one of the pool towels from the outside cabinet and dry off—twisting my pajamas to wring the water out.

I start back to the room, still toweling off my hair. There are only a few cars in the parking lot. Our car is not where we left it, and I scan the lot, looking. Then I see it, on the opposite side, and I see Mrs. Corbin sitting in the driver's seat. She doesn't see me at first—her head is down, in between her hands, which are placed on the wheel. I can feel the sorrow emanating from the car like the ripples in the pool. It is so strong it makes me sway a little as I stand there.

I walk over and knock softly on the passenger door. She looks up, startled. The car door is locked, but when I try it she pops the lock and I open it. I can't sit down right away because there are fast food wrappers strewn across the passenger seat. Mrs. Corbin looks embarrassed as she begins picking them up, putting all the trash into one of the bags. I sit down, squishing a little in my wet clothes. The car smells of grease. Her eyes are dry, but red and swollen like she has been crying for a long time.

"I'm sorry Len—I really didn't want anyone to see me like this," she says softly.

"Like what?" I ask.

She motions to the food wrappers. "I'm a mess," she says. "I'm a disgusting mess and I have absolutely no willpower. I never used to be like this. I don't even know what happened to me." Her voice is flat, tired. "I used to be normal—had to watch what I ate of course, but I was normal. Now I just can't control it. And I am like a monster—I can't fit anywhere anymore. I am always just too big. People look at me, and they just see a mess."

"I feel empty sometimes," I say.

She turns her puffy eyes to look at me, her face questioning.

"When I think about my dad. I feel hollow—like someone reached inside me and scooped everything out like a pumpkin on Halloween." I shrug. "I never thought of trying to fill up that hole with french fries, but when I think about it, it doesn't sound like too bad an idea to me."

She pulls a tissue out of a tiny little travel package and wipes her eyes.

"I don't think you're a mess, Mrs. Corbin," I say. "I think you being big like you are makes you look like nobody's gonna mess with you. Little and scrawny like me means people can just go on and do anything—it's all just gonna happen to me. But you are mighty. You are a Force to be Reckoned With."

She smiles at that one. "A force to be reckoned with, huh?" The ends of her mouth turn down in thought and she nods. "Yes, I like that Len," she says.

Neither of us makes a move to head back to bed. She hands me a full packet of French fries and she munches on another. We sit in that car and watch the sun come up. Once it's up in the sky, we crumple up those fast-food wrappers, swipe the crumbs out of the car, and sneak back into the room.

CHAPTER 52
Len (2001)

The drive home is quiet. Like really, unhealthy quiet. We stop for gas, and I switch to the front seat so Mrs. Corbin can lie down in the back. I understand why she is so tired. I turn on the radio and flip through stations. There is mostly static—the only stations coming in strong are the ones in Spanish and the one that plays different decades of music. Just my luck they are playing 80's hour. I know how Ma is. She loves this music—usually she gets a wistful smile on her face and won't let me change the station. But today when I turn it on her eyes go moist and she turns the dial herself.

Ma is lost in her own world, Mrs. Corbin snores gently in the back, and I am left thinking about things. I glance in the side mirror, get a glimpse of my strong cheekbones, my hair falling across my face. I think back to when Rachel picked up the phone to call her dad, and I remember all those things I wanted to say to her. I take a moment now to say them to myself. I tell myself that I am enough. I would love to have a daddy to teach me things, to make me laugh, to pick me up when I fall down. But I know, if I look inside deep enough, that I do not need someone else. I don't need my daddy to love me, to know that I am loved. I have Ma and Granny and Bo and Walter, and never has a girl been loved more fiercely than by those four people right there. And I know, that in the worst of times, I can pick myself up off the ground all by myself. I do not need anyone else to do it for me. I know in that moment, that I am enough.

It's a long time before we turn down the driveway to Rachel's house. The sun sits low slung in the sky by then and the clouds are rolling in. Ma parks and we get out to stretch. Mrs. Corbin gets her bag out of the trunk and we all hug goodbye. It is only then that we notice Rachel, sitting on the front porch, watching us.

"Rachel!" Mrs. Corbin gasps when she sees her. "Thank God, I've been so worried about you, honey."

Rachel rolls her eyes. "I'm fine. Dad just had something he had to do is all."

"What do you mean he had something to do? Why would he come all the way to Houston to get you and take you away from me then?"

Rachel shrugs. "I don't know." But her eyes fill with tears and she does not look as tough as usual.

Mrs. Corbin moves to sit beside her.

I walk over and squeeze Rachel's hand. "Well, my dad's still more crappy than your dad, if that makes you feel any better."

"Len," Ma says, widening her eyes.

"What?" I say. "It's true. I'm just trying to make Rach feel better." Because there is no way around it, having a dad that only wants you sometimes might suck, but it's still gotta be better than having a dad that doesn't want you at all.

"He got all mad," Rachel says quietly. "He wanted me to go all the way back to Lubbock with him and live there with him instead of you. When I said I wasn't sure, he got mad and dropped me off here."

"How long have you been here?"

"Just since last night. I didn't have my key, and I didn't want to break a window, so I just slept out here."

"Oh, Honey," Mrs. Corbin reaches over and hugs her. Not just a little wimpy arm around the shoulders, but a big, hearty hug. Rachel turns in and puts her head on her mom's shoulder and I can tell she is crying. Ma gives Mrs. Corbin a look and motions that we are going to go. She mouths a "thanks" and waves a little. Ma puts Mrs. Corbin's bag on the porch, and we pull out of the drive and head for home.

CHAPTER 53

Jean (2001)

The house I shared with Roger is the same. But I am different. I drive up to it with Ma in the passenger seat so she can supervise this 'visit' with Lucas who wants to see me here so he can spend time in his room and among the things he grew up with. As I pull into the gravel driveway and park the car, what hits me is that I really don't have a happy time I can remember here. There were moments when I was happy. Moments I thought my life was good and things were going to turn around and get better. Moments when I believed Roger and I were having fun and loved each other. But those moments always came crashing down, and that crash ruins the whole memory. We'd go out to dinner on a date night or with friends and have a lovely time, talking and laughing, and I'd think my life was good, my marriage was good. But every time, we'd come home, and suddenly Roger would be angry about something. There was a mess in the kitchen, or I had said something in front of our friends that he thought wasn't supportive enough or made him sound bad. What I remember most in this house is walking on eggshells—never having the happy, laughing home I wanted with Lucas's friends over— always letting Roger do things the way he wanted, always pushing myself down to keep the peace.

When I walk in the front door and look around it is the same. The living room furniture that we couldn't really afford but that Roger wanted, the kitchen cabinets that I wanted to just repaint myself but never did because Roger didn't think I'd do a good job. There is nothing here that makes me happy— there is no corner of this house that I feel is truly mine. It's sad to think I spent fifteen years of my life here and every memory I have is tinged with sadness and regret.

I don't want to be in the living room. I walk right past it, not even looking at the carpet to see if the blood stain is there or not. I've come early so I could go through my drawers. I have no intention of coming back to this house again after this, no matter how much Lucas might want to, and so I've brought boxes for anything I want to keep.

Ma heads to the kitchen to make some tea, and I head to the bedroom, pull out my things from the closet and quickly fill the boxes I've brought. I don't take everything. There is only so much I want to keep. I pretty much clean out my dresser drawers though—for some reason I want to clear those out. And as I am doing that, I remember the box in the closet that Roger got furious about when I moved once. I never touched it after that day, but I think about it now. I look at my watch and I still have forty minutes before Lucas is set to be here. I close my dresser and head back to the closet. On the top shelf of Roger's side there is a cardboard box. I pull it out and settle down cross legged on the floor with the box in front of me.

It's not sealed. The flaps are simply folded together so it stays shut. They're worn, so it is easy to unfold them. It's hard for me—even now my muscles tense thinking about Roger's reaction if he knew I opened his box. I have to remind myself we are way past all that and it doesn't matter to me what his reaction would be.

The box is only half full. I pull out a thick stack of letters, a small pile of photographs, and some photo albums at the very bottom. The albums are of him when he was little, and I wonder why he would leave them in the bottom of a box like that. I put them aside and pick up the stack of photos— there are the women staring back at me—there are not many, a handful of photos really. Roger and a brunette smiling at a dinner table together, Roger and a blond outside in the snow, smiling for the camera. The women are young, not beautiful but sort of pretty. Young mostly. I am not surprised. And I don't feel much of anything looking at those photographs.

Next, I pick up the letters, and I only read one. I recognize the woman's name, she worked with Roger at the plant for a bit. And I can see from the letter that he told her he was about to inherit a good deal of money and that he was in the middle of getting a divorce. I actually feel a bit sorry for the woman—I wonder how it ended between them. I don't open the others, I just thumb through them until I see one that is not addressed to Roger. It is not in an envelope, it's just a paper folded into thirds, and it has someone else's name written on the outside. That one I open, and I read. I walk slowly, sadly, over to my purse in the hallway and I put the letter inside. I will need to deliver that one later.

I finish boxing up everything I want to take with me, and I'm sitting with Ma having a cup of tea when Roger's mother drives up and Lucas gets out of the car. I watch from the kitchen window as he shuts the door behind him and doesn't look back. He doesn't know I am watching and my heart flies up in my chest a little when I see him smile. He smiles like when he was little, and I would pick him up after preschool. Like he has missed me all day and is so happy to see his mommy again. I grab a tissue to dab my eyes as I walk to the front door. Ma has already headed out to the garden to give us a little space.

By the time I open the door, his face is drawn and he won't look at me. I reach out to him and hug him anyway. He doesn't hug me back, but he doesn't pull away either.

"I wanna get some things from my room," he says, and he starts down the hall.

"Okay," I say. I wait, and I'm just about to follow him over and into his room when he comes back down the hall carrying his Gameboy and a handful of game cartridges.

"Come sit with me, honey," I say.

He shrugs and follows me into the kitchen and plops down at the table looking down at his game.

"So, I need to talk to you about all this—about me and your dad—about how things were between us."

He keeps looking down. He is quiet, but I know he's listening.

"I'm sure you know I found him with another woman. There's no excuse for what I did—I'm not trying to make any excuses. But I want you to understand some things about your father so that he doesn't hurt you the way he hurt me. And we need to get someone to help us talk about it. Someone who knows a lot about this sort of stuff."

"You want me to see a shrink?"

"A counselor. We'll go together."

"Why do I have to go? I'm not the crazy one."

"Neither of us is crazy. But things in our house were more complicated than I realized."

Finally he nods, looking resigned.

We don't actually do much for the rest of our visit. He lets me watch him while he plays his game boy and I try to get him to talk to me about school. It doesn't matter. I am sitting here in the same room with him for the whole time, and that is all that matters to me.

When his grandmother's car pulls into the drive and she honks, he actually looks sad. At the doorway I pull him in for a hug and for a brief moment, he hugs me back. He walks out the door, but just outside he turns back. "I don't know about all this stuff, but I do know this Ma—Dad can be an asshole sometimes."

I nod. "Yeah. That's for damn sure."

CHAPTER 54

Cora (2001)

C ora is in the garden before sunrise, as she has been every morning since she returned from Houston. She kneels, as the sun climbs in the sky, letting the light enter her, fill her. She breathes in the earth scent, plucks a tiny weed from the well-tilled bed. The earth is ready to burst forth with life, she can tell. Earlier she filled her wheelbarrow with thick, heavy soil from the compost pile, picking off the mushrooms that had started to take hold on the shady side. The silt feeling of it, the smell of the churned soil calms her now, as she tries to push all thoughts of the trip, all thoughts of seeing him, out of her head.

As she works, she lets her mind wander to the sticky part of her thesis. She has been trying to reconcile Kierkegaard's understanding of existentialism as individualism concerned with free choice—decisions that require leaps of faith -- with Hegel's systematizing ambitions and his metaphysics of Geist. She feels she can add something new to the discussion, she is sure of it. But every time she gets close to something it slips away. Usually gardening helps, and typically she would emerge with at least a new idea to try. But even after an hour of pruning and fertilizing, letting her mind mull over the incongruities of the positions, Cora still has not had the epiphany she's been waiting for. Everything she comes up with sounds like the Hallmark inspirationalism of a Mitch Albom novel instead of the answer to an esoteric philosophical dilemma she has been grappling with for nearly two years now. She knows she is making too much of Pavlov, and that there has to be more room for hope.

Cora knows that before she can publish her writing, she'll need to finish her degree. If she does that, she could teach. She wants to do both - she wants to finish the work she is doing, not just seal it up in a musty doctoral thesis that will never see the light of day. She wants to bring the theories she loves into the light, make them resonate with regular people, not only with people who sit in stuffy libraries all day wearing tweed jackets and talking about tenure. Now that Len is older, it's time to think about moving. Given the circumstances, it would help them both to get a fresh start. She knows it won't be easy, but it is time.

Cora hears the car before she sees it, and when it comes into view, snaking down the long driveway toward her, she stands, wipes the dirt off her hands onto her work rag and shields her face from the sun with her hand. Tires crunch on gravel as the car pulls to the end of the drive.

For a moment Cora doesn't recognize the lady who gets out. She's filled out a little, but instead of appearing heavier, Jean Goodson looks light and airy walking up the driveway toward her. Cora wipes her hands again on her rag.

Cora has always found Jean reserved and bit morose. Okay, if she's completely honest with herself, she's always found her a little boring. She's quiet, doesn't say much, almost never laughs.

Jean gives her a wide smile as she approaches. She lifts her head to take in the blue Texas sky and the mountains far behind the farm. "I never get used to how beautiful it is. Right out here in our own backyard and I just took it all for granted."

Cora reaches out to embrace her. "I'm surprised to see you," she says. "I knew you were getting," she pauses for a moment, stuck and uncomfortable, "back," she continues. "I just didn't know when."

Jean laughs. "You can go on and say it. Lord knows it ain't no secret where I been lately. I didn't get back—I got out." She looks at Cora purposefully. "That is a world of difference right there."

"Well, you look good, Jean. You look really good."

Jean laughs again. "Yeah, you know your life is just about as messed up as it can get when spending a few months in prison is actually a good thing for you."

"Come on in, I'll get us some iced tea."

"How are you?" Cora asks as they sit in the living room a few minutes later, tall glasses of tea sweating on the coffee table.

Jean shrugs. "Well, I'm out, that's the main thing. They say Roger's gonna be fine. That's how come I got out of course. His family said they didn't want some long, drawn-out trial. They say he's home with his ma, recovering still."

"You haven't seen him?"

She shakes her head. "You know, I really just didn't know how messed up we got together—dysfunctional—that's what the prison shrink called it. When I look back, it seems so obvious, but somehow I had no idea. I always ended up believing that I was the messed up one." She shakes her head again. "I reckon I was 'dysfunctional' in my own way, otherwise I never would have put up with it all. But he could be very convincing the way he put things."

"I heard a few things," Cora says. "Did he hit you Jean? Was he abusing you?" Cora can't believe that she wouldn't have known that.

Jean shakes her head. "He never hit me. I think if he had, in a weird messed up way it would have been better. I would have known what it was then. It would have been easy to identify. Maybe not easy to leave, but I would have done it." She is quiet for a moment. "At least I think I would have. I like to think I would have."

Jean reaches into the bag beside her and pulls out an envelope. "I found something. I was going through a box of Roger's things that somehow got left behind when his ma came to take everything away."

Jean has the saddest look. "I don't even know what to say about this Cora, how sorry I am that he kept it." She turns the envelope over in her hands and Cora sees her own name written on the outside. "I read it. I didn't know what it was of course, so I read it. I don't even know what to say. Just, I'm so, so sorry."

Cora takes the envelope. She doesn't recognize the handwriting on the front. She opens it and reads.

Dear Cora,

I don't have a lot of time, so I hope this comes out right the first time I try to put it down on paper. I got a call from my agent—there's this audition he thinks could be my big break. It's in six hours so I only have time to throw all my stuff in a bag and hit the road. I called, but you were out and I can't leave a message on your machine because I don't want your Mom to think I'm a psycho.

Here's the thing. I am rushing around finding all my stuff to pack, and I should be elated. This audition could be huge for me—this could be the start of everything. I should feel like I am flying toward my future. But I don't. I feel like my limbs are moving through water, like everything is heavy and difficult. I don't feel like my future is in Dallas, because you are here in Abilene.

When you asked me last night if I loved you, I hesitated. It wasn't because I wasn't feeling it, it was because I was feeling too much. I've never felt like this before about anyone—not even close, and I don't know how to say it without sounding like a lunatic.

I know you have to go back to Georgetown in the fall. But here's the thing - it doesn't really matter where I am at the moment. As long as I can buy a bus ticket to get to auditions, I'm free to go where I want. See, when I write it that way I worry I sound a bit crazy, a bit clingy—like here we've just started dating and I want to come live with you across the country. Maybe I'm just a sappy romantic at heart and I just didn't even know it until now. I'd like to sound a little cooler at the moment, a little more like I don't care, but I do.

Will you just come meet me in Dallas? At least do that—we can worry about the rest of it all later. I know it's too soon for me to lay all this heavy stuff on you, but when I picture my future, however I picture it turning out, you're in it.

I am packing my bags, but at the moment I don't really want to go off and follow my dreams, I just want to sit on the porch holding your hand and watching the sunset.

I'm leaving you my parent's number. Even if you can't make it to Dallas, they'll know how to reach me. I'm also going to give you an out. I'm going to force myself not to call you, so that if you get this and are totally freaked out because it is just way too much, you can just bow out gracefully.

But I sure hope you call. I'll be waiting.

Love,
Edison

Below his signature is his parents' name and number. Full name, including his last name—Dean.

Cora is still. Everything around her and inside of her is frozen as the implications of what she just read fall slowly, unbelievably into place for her. She feels gutted, hollowed out, as if her entire life to this point has been a lie. She feels, so vividly now, the same raw pain she had originally felt in those days when she was curled up and crying at the loss of him. She feels the betrayal all over again, just as it had been at the time—more deeply than anything she had ever felt before except the death of her father. And suddenly now, with this new information, the moments of her life shift somehow. She thinks of those beautiful moments with Len—in the hospital when she was born, watching her first steps, her first words, but then seeing those other couples out and about smiling together at their children and feeling stabbed in the heart every time. Every premise she's held about why her life is the way it is now shifts—like a kaleidoscope turning so that the pieces are the same, but now form a completely different picture.

Cora sits, finding it difficult to breath, difficult to speak. Her surroundings have evaporated, and there is only the piece of paper in her hand and the stark reality of what it means. He hadn't left her as she thought all these years. She looks at Jean and tries to speak, at first only opening and closing her mouth.

"How did Roger have this? Why would he keep this from me?"

Jean shakes her head. "I don't know."

"Oh my God!" Cora's voice gets louder as the reality sinks in. Her stunned, punched-in-the-gut feeling is giving way to anger now. "My whole life! How the fuck?"

Jean reaches out and touches Cora's shoulder. "I'm so sorry."

Cora doesn't know Jean's whole story, but she knows instinctively that the same man has stolen both of their lives.

She reads the letter again. Those feelings are there inside her still, after all this time muted by hurt and time and experience, but they are there. Cora is all of a sudden twenty again. She can feel the touch of his hand on her face, the heat of his body as he pulled her to him, the complete abandon in which she had lost herself so completely and utterly.

"Oh my God!" she says again.

Jean nods. What could be said about it, really?

"Well, let me tell you something—I sure as hell have a new understanding of your predicament," Cora says. "Roger was the one who picked up the phone when I called." She remembers now. "He was the one who told me Edison left and didn't leave me a message."

Jean nods. "I wish I could say I'm surprised." She stands. "I should go. I am so sorry to be the one to bring this to you."

Cora is in a daze as she says goodbye. She's still in a daze as she sits on the wide windowsill in the living room watching the car snake back out the driveway, the breeze blowing the leaves of the banana tree. She sits there for a long time.

By the time Len and Granny come through the door, Cora is sitting beside the ancient record player she's dragged out of the attic, her entire vinyl album collection splayed out in front of her, while Sisters of Mercy plays over and over again at high volume—"First and Last and Always." Cora's eyes are red and puffy as she flips through the record jackets. Joy Division, PIL,

General Public. She'd listened to "Tenderness" over and over again. It always touched a nerve, always reminded her of him.

She is suddenly brought back to the present by Len standing in front of her.

"Uh, Ma? Are you OK?"

She looks at her daughter and aches for all the Father-Daughter dances missed at school, for every Father's Day filled with a dull emptiness instead of a messy child-made breakfast in bed and a crayon-drawing card. She feels with a keenness that empty spot inside of her daughter where a father's love should lie. And as she looks at Len's strong, worried face, her eyes fill with tears again.

"Granny, do you want to make some special tea or something? I think Ma's losing it." But Len says it gently and bends down to hug Cora as if Len were the parent comforting her child.

Cora pulls herself together as Granny turns off the record player. "I'm okay, really. I…" But she can't quite finish her sentence.

Len raises her eyebrows, her gaze skeptical.

They sit in the kitchen, Cora drinking the steaming mug of spicy tea her mother sets in front of her. She takes the letter from her pocket, where she's folded it so many times that she now regrets it and smooths it out, trying to flatten the folds.

"Here," she says to both of them, to her daughter and mother at once. She holds it out to them as if this is the answer to everything—to the multitude of questions that are at the moment unspoken. Like 'what the heck is your problem, you need to think about your daughter here?' which is emanating from the both of them.

Len picks up the paper. "What's this?"

"Jean brought it over. She found it with Roger's things."

"But it's to you," Len says, glancing at the page. "It says Dear Cora."

Cora nods. "Just read it."

Cora watches her as she does. For the second time in many years, Cora wants to take something, some kind of pill. She wants the freedom to leave her body, to not be responsible. She wants to feel like there is something bigger than her—like she is only a tiny cog in the enormous wheel of the cosmos. She does not want to be sloppy drunk. But given the contents of the house, she knows that would be a much more realistic goal. She pushes her tea away, stands up and goes to the liquor cabinet.

If only she liked the taste of whiskey. The romance of it, the raw harshness of just pouring some gut rotting liquid in a glass, swirling it around a few times and swigging it down. It seems the perfect drink for misery, and she wants to wallow completely. But when she opens the bottle, even the smell of it makes her gag, so she replaces it and pours herself a glass of vodka. She adds tonic and ice and gulps half of it down immediately.

The image that she cannot let go of is of Len when she was a baby. How happy Cora would be in those moments when she was nursing Len, or rocking her to sleep, or quietly playing with her on the floor. But always those moments contained the absence of Edison.

She'd always pushed those thoughts away when they came to her over the years. Things happen in life, she'd remind herself. It's never perfect, never a fairy tale ending. People get divorced, people die, people fall out of love. She had known she could not expect life to be perfect, and that she would have to let go of those dreams of a postcard perfect family. That ideal image she held in her mind had to shift to a new version of happiness—her and her daughter and her own family. And she'd been able to let go of so much of it. She'd been happy. But she realizes now, she had also been cheated.

Len finishes reading the note and passes it to Granny. The only sound is Cora refilling her glass.

"Roger had this the whole time?" Granny asks in disbelief. Cora nods.

"I always said that boy loved you. I always knew it."

"Well I guess that explains it." Cora tries to keep the hard edge of anger out of her voice.

Len looks at her. "You never got this?"

"No."

"So, he loved you and wanted you and you didn't know? All this time you didn't know?"

"No," she shakes her head. "All this time I didn't know."

Len is quiet for a long time, thinking. "Do you think he wanted me too?" she asks it softly, almost to herself.

Cora goes soft in an instant. What she had been robbed of was nothing compared to what had been taken from Len.

"Oh honey," she moves to her daughter and strokes her hair. What can she say to make it better? What can she possibly say?

Granny takes Len's hand and holds it fiercely. "All his life he has missed you," she says, her voice strong and sure. "All his life, he wanted to walk in the door and see his two loves. He missed those moments of coming home, walking into the room and seeing your mama sitting there in the rocking chair, holding you, or the both of you lying in bed napping, or laughing together, playing. He has felt an emptiness all his life from missing that." She squeezes Len's hand tightly. "I am never wrong about these things, just ask your mother."

CHAPTER 55
Cora (2001)

It takes Cora a few days to make the call. A few days of wallowing in self-pity, of vacillating from that to elation because after all, he did love her—at least, he had. It was years ago so of course she doesn't expect him to feel the same now. But the fact that he had loved her, that she had not been simply a notch in his belt, shifts her entire view of her life.

Here she is, in the exact same situation she had been in before she read Edison's letter, and yet her entire life is different. All because the story has changed. The facts haven't changed, only her perspective has.

She thinks for some time about whether to call or not. Edison had been quite clear that he had no interest in seeing her or Len, and Cora doesn't expect that to change. But Len has a grandmother out there and Cora owes it to her daughter to find out if that grandmother wants to be in Len's life.

She holds the phone in her hand but waits a long time before dialing. She knows the chances of the number being the same are small. Most likely Edison's parents have moved away. Perhaps they've died even, and this will all come to nothing.

"Hello, Mrs. Dean?"

The voice is guarded, worried at first. "Yes."

"My name is Coralee. I knew Edison a long time ago."

There is a pause as Cora struggles with what to say next.

"Is Edison alright? What's wrong?"

"No, Edison's fine. At least I think so, I don't know. I mean, I'm calling because he left me a letter with your number. But he left it for me a long time ago. The thing is, I never got it. I never had a number to call. I thought he just left me."

"Did you say your name was Cora?"

"Yes Ma'am."

"I remember now. He sure waited a long time to hear from you."

There is silence for a moment, but the woman's voice is kinder when she speaks again. "I think you might want to let him know that instead of me."

"Well, maybe. But I don't think he wants to hear from me. I don't think he cares any more. But I wanted to let you know." She pauses again. She wants to tell her about Len. The reason she'd called was to tell her about Len. But for some reason she can't say the words. Instead she says, "I just wanted you to know."

After she hangs up, she thinks about calling back. She will, she tells herself. She'll call back another time and tell her.

CHAPTER 56

Cora (2001)

Cora stares at the front door of the small white house. The letter, folded again with her name written on the front, is in her hand. Her fingers are white as she holds it, every muscle alight with anger, like a coil wound and ready to spring. But she hesitates. Because really, what's done is done, and she isn't sure what good it'll do to confront him now. But in the end, she decides she needs to know why. What kind of person would do this to someone? She'd never been particularly fond of Roger. She hadn't been too thrilled at becoming related to him through her brother's marriage. But she had not known he was capable of something like this.

She walks to the door, determined. But when Roger opens it, he doesn't look like the cocky bastard she expects. He is thin, gaunt even, and he leans heavily on a cane.

He doesn't say anything. For a moment he looks eager, excited even, as if he thinks perhaps she's there to give him her best wishes, say how sorry she is that he'd been injured.

She holds out the envelope.

"Hello there Cora," his voice is guarded. "So nice of you to drop by. Would you like to come in?"

"Why the hell did you do this Roger?" Her voice is constrained—poured over ice. "Why didn't you ever give this to me?"

She waives the letter, and his face hardens as he takes it in.

"I don't know what you're talking about."

"Jean brought it to me. She found it in some things you left."

He nods. "Well that explains it. Jean can be very manipulative. She's made people believe all sorts of crazy things about me. But I'm sorry she kept that letter, whatever's in it. I had no idea she had something that was so important to you." He cocks his head, looking apologetic. "She likes to stir up trouble for other people sometimes and then pretend she had nothing to do with it. I think it makes her feel better about her own sorry, sad life if other people aren't getting what they want either. If I'd known she had it of course I would have made sure she got it to you."

"You are a fucking piece of work, you know that Roger? I don't know what kind of sick satisfaction you got out of keeping this all these years, but you are some kind of fucked-up, that's for sure."

Roger smirks and holds up his hands, shrugging. "Sorry, whatever it is you think I did, I can't help you."

Cora cannot believe later, as she replays the scene in her head, that the only insult that pops into her head at this important time, is from a Pixar movie. It was Len's favorite when she was little. "You are a sad, strange little man, Roger," she says. She turns and walks back to her car. But once there she turns back around. "Don't you ever come near me or my family again. Ever."

CHAPTER 57

Cora (2001)

A t first Cora can't quite make out the figure sitting on the front steps as she drives up the driveway. She thinks at first glance it must be Bo, but Bo doesn't sit like that. When she pulls close enough, and he lifts his head so she can see his face, she stops her car right there in the middle of the driveway and tries hard to breathe. She gets out of the car and starts walking before realizing that is a really dumb thing to do because now there is this long time between getting out of the car and getting close enough to say something to him. But maybe it's a good thing after all, because she has absolutely no idea what to say.

She walks up, looks him in the eye and says, "Hi."

He doesn't say anything, just smiles. He is too much of a pretty boy for her, she's sure of it. She definitely does not need this in her life right at the moment.

"It's been a long time, Cora."

"Yeah, well if you count me seeing you in Houston, then it's really only been a couple of weeks, so…"

He smiles. "You haven't changed."

"Oh yes I have. I have changed hugely. I had to. Being a mom will do that to you."

He sits on the porch, his dark jeans faded in just the right places, vintage T shirt with a picture of Darth Vadar on it, and a braided brown leather bracelet on his wrist. She makes sure to stand at a bit of a distance. It's like there's an electric pulse emanating from him, and she's scared to get too close, scared to get caught up in the magnetism again. He looks the same, but not the same. It's strange, after all this time, to see the face she'd known so well, had dreamed about in a thousand daydreams, there in front of her but shifted, filled out a little, crinkled a little. But other than that, it's the same.

He is studying her. "You look good Cora."

She's suddenly filled with a sadness, deep and tender. He couldn't be here because of the call she'd made to his mother. There wasn't enough time for him to have gotten all the way here. He doesn't know yet.

She pulls the envelope from her pocket. "I never got the letter you wrote. I didn't even know about it until yesterday."

"What?" His whole body shifts as he takes in this news.

She holds it out in front of her. "Remember your friend Mike's roommate Roger? His wife Jean brought it to me. She found it, and she read it and she brought it to me. I just went to tell Roger off—but he's such a twisted guy, it wasn't as satisfying as I had hoped."

Edison moves so that he leans into his knees. He blows into his hands as if it's cold outside. "Jesus, are you kidding me?!"

Cora knows what it is like to get this news, to have to adjust your entire way of thinking about the past, so she gives him a minute. After a while she says, "I thought you skipped town and just left me." Later, she thinks, she will tell him how she called and talked to Roger, how she searched for him in every phone book, in every way she could, all the ways she looked for him over the years. "Did you know, all that time we spent together, and I never even asked your last name. It made it hard to find you that's for sure."

Edison shakes his head. "All this time, I thought…"

"I know," Cora says.

"Why'd you come here?" she asks softly -- not accusing, just wondering. "What made you come?"

"Well, as my assistant so wisely said, 'you can hate that lady all you want to, but anybody can see that girl is your daughter.'" His eyes are sad. Cora knows there is so much he has missed out on, so much he can never get back. She hadn't thought about it, but perhaps Roger's betrayal cost Edison more than it had cost her. He would never hold his baby, never rock her to sleep or feed her a bottle.

"Len's at a friend's house. She'll be back a little later." She's not quite sure what to do next. "You want to come in?" she asks. "I'll show you pictures."

Cora does not sit next to him. She's scared to be too close. It feels as if having him here is a dream and he will vanish the moment she's pulled back to reality. Edison sits on the sofa, the hanging violet creeping down and hovering just over his shoulder, while Cora pulls out Len's baby book. She hands it to him. He runs his hand over the old-fashioned leather cover. It had been a gift from Tessa, so classic that it was like and unlike her at the same time. There's an embossed picture of a silver rattle and teething ring on the front.

Slowly Edison opens the book. There is Len as a tiny pea pod in the hospital, with Cora young and fresh and smiling. Len sleeping in her crib, being held by Granny, Len sitting in her highchair, face covered in spaghetti. He sees her first birthday, her second, her first day of kindergarten, and the gap tooth smile of the first lost tooth.

When he looks up at Cora, his eyes are moist. "I don't know what to do now," he says.

Cora doesn't know either. She shrugs. "Let's have a drink."

"It's 11:00 in the morning."

"Shit, I've just had my whole entire world pulled out from under my feet—you've just seen—God, it's ridiculous what we've been through, I think we deserve to let ourselves have a fucking drink if we want."

"You really haven't changed, no matter what you say." He smiles. "Okay, let's have a drink."

When she looks at the liquor cabinet though, she knows that vodka will make her cry. Eventually, Tequila will make her cry too, and so will gin. Then she remembers the bottle in the fridge, bought and placed there in anticipation of her finishing her thesis.

When she comes back in the room holding the bottle and two champagne flutes, she realizes this does not look the way she wanted it to. She wishes she was holding a bottle of whiskey instead. "I just don't have anything else to drink—sorry." She shrugs. "It is not a celebration, it's just a drink."

She pops the cork and pours the glasses. They drink in silence for a moment and then he says "So, what's new in your life?"

She looks at him like he's crazy.

"I just mean, how are you Cora?"

Still, she gives the crazy look.

"You look good," he tries again.

"I don't look good," Cora says. "I look like a Mom."

"Maybe a Mom can look good," he says.

He pours more champagne, and she finds another bottle in the wine rack in the basement.

She has to pretend there is a buffer around him, a safe zone. She does not want to get any nearer to him than the safe zone, for she knows she can't be held responsible for whatever might happen next. One moment she looks at him and she barely recognizes him. He is from some distant, long ago point in her life. But the next moment she looks at him and it is as if no time has passed at all since that summer.

Once he starts with the 'do you remembers,' it's all over for her. Do you remember how we went to that drive-in? Do you remember Tuesdays at the Upstairs Lounge?

"I remember everything," she says. "I remember every single moment, like it was yesterday. I remember every time you kissed me, every word you said to me, exactly how it felt when you held me."

He reaches out for her, cups her face in his hand, its warmth filling her.

"Me too," he says.

CHAPTER 58

Len (2001)

I haven't seen Rachel much in the couple of weeks since our trip to nowhere. I haven't felt like hanging out at the pool or the mall, or doing much of anything really. But I am worried about school starting next week. She's a grade ahead of me, which in middle school is pretty much like being in an entirely different universe. And I miss her.

I walk up the porch steps and ring the bell. As soon as Mrs. Corbin opens the door, I can tell that things are not good over here. She is wearing an old, worn-out bathrobe, her hair limp and greasy. I am betting she hasn't showered since we got back from Houston.

"Hi Mrs. Corbin," I say, trying to pretend things seem normal. "Is Rachel here?"

"No," she says, looking down. "I'm sorry Len, she's not here."

"Well, do you know when she'll be home? I can come back."

She shakes her head again. "I don't know if she's coming back."

"What?" I say. "What do you mean?"

"Some lady from social services came over. Told me someone called with a concern that they saw a girl sleeping on the porch and were worried for her welfare or some crap like that. They wouldn't tell me who called, but I know it was him."

I raise my eyebrows in surprise, and she goes on.

"She wanted to 'inspect the home'—that's how she said it. So I let her in. I told her we were still just moving in, that's why it was a bit of a mess at the moment. But I don't think she believed me, or maybe she is just—I don't know what it was, but she made little marks on her paper as she walked around the place and then they took Rachel away."

"Where'd they take her?" I ask in disbelief.

She shakes her head. "If I know her father, I bet you anything he has talked them into letting her go live with him."

"But her dad is mean," I say.

"I know," Mrs. Corbin says. "But I guess the state of Texas don't really care so much about that. Ain't no law against being mean. But there must be a law against being messy I guess, so…"

I feel her sadness.

"I don't feel so much like a Force to be Reckoned With at the moment, honey, that's for sure," she says.

I nod. "This sucks."

She laughs. "Well, that is a good way of putting it. I couldn't have said it better myself."

"Don't you even get to talk to the judge about this?" I ask, remembering that she has a court order and all.

She nods. "Yes. I do. But this is what they call 'exigent circumstances' which I guess means they can do what they want until I get to go into court. I'll go down to the courthouse on Monday, but it is always weeks away when they set that hearing in front of the judge."

"Well, it's not my place to say, Mrs. Corbin, but it seems to me that what you need is a really good lawyer."

She nods. "Yeah, maybe if I win the lottery I can afford one of those."

I turn to go. "Let us know if there is anything we can do." That sentence is my mama coming out of me—I hear it as soon as I say it. But I know it is a good thing to say, so I let it float there between us as I walk back home.

I can feel something electric in the air as soon as I get close enough to see our house. I don't know what it is—I can't place the feeling, can't even tell whether it is good or bad. But it is strong—magnetic, pulling me in and pulling me apart at the same time. I spot the car in the driveway, so I know someone else is there, but nothing prepares me for the sight I see when I walk in the door.

There is my daddy, sitting there clear as day, in the middle of my living room. Ma is with him, her cheeks flushed, a champagne glass in her hand. It is almost unbelievable. I have spent my whole life looking for my daddy, dreamin' about him, and then all of sudden here he is right here in front of me. I have no idea what to do.

There is a photo album between them, one cover on Ma's knee, the other on his. When Ma sees me she stands up. "Len, honey, there is someone I want you to meet."

But I am not looking at her. I am staring at him. He looks at me this time, not like before. He really looks at me and I see in his face a mixture of sadness, regret, and even a little anger, although I know it is not anger at me.

Ma wobbles a little.

"Are you drunk?" I ask, incredulous.

But it doesn't matter.

He smiles at me. "Hi Len," he says. "I think it's about time we met properly."

I don't know what to do. I try to smile at him, light and cheery like a happy daughter that he will want. But instead I make a sort of choking noise, and big fat tear drops start rolling down my face. My face crinkles up all ugly as I try to stop myself from crying. That is not how this was supposed to go. I get scared, because he was already pretty prone to flight, and why is he gonna want to stay here and get to know me if I just stand here and ball like a baby.

But instead of heading for the door, he walks toward me. He reaches his arms around me, gentle and strong, and pulls me to him in a hug. He pats my back and says, "It's okay. That's how most women react when they meet me."

I laugh a little through my tears and wipe my eyes. But he doesn't let go. He holds me, safe and protected. And I reach up and put my arms around him and hug him back. As I do, I feel a little jolt of energy—it is like it is being pulled right out of my chest. I can see it in the air even. There is nothing solid to see, but it is a shimmer, a vibration really, and I watch it leave me and float in the air just a little bit, hovering, before it floats gently out the window and up into the sky.

The next morning, the darkness is gone. I don't realize it at first; Walter hands me a corn fritter, warm and greasy, and we watch the moon for a little while. It shines, full and bright even as the first fingers of dawn creep into the sky.

"Well Pea," Walter says, "How 'bout that? After all this time." He puts his hand on my shoulder. "I sure am sorry he didn't come sooner," he says.

I remember all the times Walter picked me up and dusted me off when I was learning to ride, all the times he sat and listened to me as I told him about what had happened at school—how I didn't fit in, or how I wanted to be like the other girls whose dads picked them up from school and took them to soccer practice. I remember him looking right into my eyes and telling me, "You don't want to be like all those other girls. You're special—why would you ever want to be just like everyone else?"

I reach up and take Walter's hand. "Yeah," I say. "Me too."

When I ride the perimeter that morning, there is only regular sky. There is no darkness, there is no threat. I even back track a few times, to make sure I'm not missing anything. But there is nothing there. Cyclops and I have nothing to do.

When we get back to the barn though, and I am about to tell Walter, the words stop in my throat. I watch him, stooped and slow, as he goes about his work, and my heart aches just a little. I untack Cyclops, brush him and make sure there is water in his stall. Before I leave the barn, I give Walter a big hug, holding him just long enough for him to look down at me and say, "What's all this about then?"

"Nothin'," I say, letting him go and heading back to the house. I will see him tomorrow morning, same time. Before then, I will see my father again.

Cora watches her daughter walking back from the barn. She walks straight and tall and strong, and Cora can tell that something has changed. It changed the moment Len hugged her father. There was a shift in the air, some electric current shot through the room. Cora knew it, she just didn't know what it meant.

But she isn't worried. She has known her daughter was special from the moment she was born. Some people are born tall, some short, some smart, some beautiful. Len, she knows, was just born a little bit different.

SPECIAL THANKS

My heartfelt thanks to the following:

M. Scott Douglass at The Main Street Rag, for taking a chance on a debut author, and for believing in this book enough to see it to the finish line.

Jennifer Thompson and Isabelle Bleeker of Nordlyset Literary Agency, for your unwavering support of this novel, and for sticking by me through thick and thin. It has meant the world to me.

My teachers and mentors at Fairfield, for your wisdom, guidance, and for the supportive community you have created that endures long after graduation. In particular, Karen Osborn and Rachel Basch—thank you for going above and beyond in support of me and my work. Also to Eugenia Kim, Susan Muaddi Darraj, and Ladee Hubbard. And to all my cohort and classmates, in particular, Kathleen B. Jones, Alanna Johnson, Christina Simpson, Madeline Deluca, and Nicole Heller.

To my sisters in this writing life—Susan Bien, Sally Pla, Ona Russel, and Sarah Sleeper—my first and best readers, and the most supportive group of writers and friends I could ever wish for. You guys have been there for everything—the ups and downs, the really very far downs, the struggles, and the celebrations—I would never have made it this far without you.

My kids—Evan, Isabel, Oliver, and Emily—who are my whole heart, my biggest cheering section, and without a doubt my crowning achievement.

All my family and friends for the love and support you've shown me over the years, but even more than that, for living life with me in all its imperfect glory—thank you for taking me along on this journey.